Ride Out to Vengeance

Swift, deadly and merciless were the raiders who hit the Kansas ranch and when they had rode out they left behind two men dead and a woman who wouldn't make it through the night. With a stolen Army payroll in their saddlebags they ran for the border and although they covered their back trail well, someone was on it. He was a man with a gun, determined to hunt every one of them down. His name was Angel and the name of his game was sudden death.

And so the Justice Department put their best man into the field with one simple instruction. Before he kills every one of them – find ANGEL!

By the same author

Standoff at Liberty

Ride Out to Vengeance

Daniel Rockfern

A Black Horse Western

ROBERT HALE · LONDON

© 1973, 2005 Frederick Nolan
First hardcover edition 2005
Originally published in paperback as
Find Angel by Frederick H. Christian

ISBN 0 7090 7631 2

Robert Hale Limited
Clerkenwell House
Clerkenwell Green
London EC1R 0HT

Typeset by
Derek Doyle & Associates, Liverpool.
Printed and bound in Great Britain by
Antony Rowe Limited, Wiltshire

A NOTE TO
THE READER

In Record Group 60 of the National Archives in Washington DC there is abundant documentary evidence to the effect that for a number of years the United States Department of Justice employed a Special Investigator named Frank Angel, who was directly responsible to the Attorney-General of the United States. There is no record that the events portrayed in this book took place, or that Frank Angel took part in them. Equally, there is no record that he did not.

ONE

There were seven of them.

Three days earlier they had ambushed a paymaster's wagon on its way to Fort Riley, killing the four troopers riding escort and a civilian teamster, a Swede named Soderstrom. Then they headed out hard and fast across the flat empty Kansas plain, quartering south and west, keeping away from the settlements and the Army posts where the telegraph would have already chattered with the news of the robbery, moving steadily towards the Colorado border.

Now they crested a bluff about ten miles beyond Fort Dodge, skirting along its northern side down into a broad valley. Below them they could see smoke rising from the chimney of a ranch standing shaded in a grove of stunted cottonwoods. In the sturdily-built corrals, horses stood hip-shot in the flat morning sun.

'How many miles to the border?' the leader said.

' 'Bout forty miles to the Cimarron,' someone answered.

'We need fresh horses,' the leader said.

The seven men moved down the side of the valley and came up to the ranch. They were shaggy and unkempt after three days' hard riding, and the horses were just about finished.

A man came out of the house and stood in the yard, shading his eyes against the sunlight with his hand. He looked to be about thirty, but you couldn't tell in this country.

'Howdy, all,' he said as the riders bunched up before him in the yard.

'You boys look like you come a far piece.'

'That we have,' said the leader of the riders. As he dismounted it became clear that his huge shoulders, thick neck and barrel chest were oddly out of proportion with the rest of his body, for he was a short man who walked with an almost nautical roll. He slapped the dust from his clothes with his Stetson and extended a hand.

'Cravetts is my name,' he said. He had a good smile. 'Me an' the boys here are on our way back to Farmington in New Mex. Just delivered us a herd in Sedalia and happy to be done with her. Can't get back to the little woman fast enough.'

'Know how you feel,' the rancher said. 'Glad to know you, Cravetts. My name's John Gibbons. Run this place with m'wife, couple o' hands.'

'Nice spread,' nodded Cravetts. 'You run many head?'

'Few hundred,' Gibbons replied. 'Mostly it's horses. We got a good deal goin' with the so'jer boys, over at Dodge an' Larned. Take all the animals we can give 'em.'

Cravetts exchanged a glance with his men, who had dismounted too and were standing in almost posed indolence in a half circle behind him.

'How many horses you got here now? he asked.

'Twenty, mebbe,' Gibbons said. 'But listen, let's get in out of this sun. I guess you men wouldn't say no to some coffee?'

'That's raht frien'ly o' you, mister,' said one of the men, a tall tow-haired fellow of maybe twenty-three or four. 'We'd sure appreciate it.'

'You boys can take your coffee out here,' Cravetts said. 'We're travelling pretty light, Mr Gibbons, an' as fast as we can. Don't want the boys dirtying up your missus' house.'

At that moment, Mrs Gibbons came to the door, a clutch of tin cups and a coffeepot in her hands. Cravetts hastened to help her, and she smiled her thanks. She was a young woman, her blonde hair tied back with a piece of checkered gingham, and there were dimples in her cheeks.

'You gentlemen come on up here and get your coffee,' she said, and nodded to each one as Cravetts introduced them.

'Lee Monsher,' he said, as the tow-haired youngster with the Southern accent took his cup. 'Howie Kamins, Frank Torelli, Johnnie Vister, Milt Sharp, and Denny Juba.'

'You boys are some ways off the main trail,' Gibbons remarked.

Monsher's head came up at the words, but a glance from Cravetts stilled the movement, and the wary look in Monsher's eyes was hooded quickly.

'We're carrying a fair piece of money, Mr Gibbons,' Cravetts said. 'I figured it was best to stay off the beaten path a little.'

'You might be right at that,' Gibbons said. He sipped his coffee and his eyes touched the grouped men squatting drinking. Cravetts marked how the rancher ticked off the fact that all of the men were heavily armed, and he could see Gibbons trying to frame a question that would satisfy his curiosity without appearing rude or prying.

'You run this place with just two hands,' he said. 'Must keep you pretty occupied.'

'It has its moments,' Gibbons said.

9

'Your boys around?' Cravetts asked.

'Dave is in the barn,' Gibbons said. 'Frank—' His eyes arrowed.

Cravetts saw it and knew that in that moment Gibbons had put together all the questions he had asked and come up with the reason for them and without another thought Cravetts shot the rancher through the heart. The rancher reeled backwards, his chest smashed in by the heavy calibre bullet, his shirt smouldering. Mrs Gibbons screamed, whirling around so that the coffee spewed from the pot in a steaming tan arc, and her scream was still hanging in the air as a youngster came out of the barn, running with his head up and a cocked sixgun in his hand. Cravetts' men were on their feet now and three of them fired almost simultaneously, the bullets whipping the boy off his feet and smashing him into the dirt of the yard, scattering the chickens foraging there.

'Check it out!' snapped Cravetts, gesturing towards the house, and Monsher and two of the others ran inside, guns drawn, as Torelli and Vister grappled with Mrs Gibbons, who was trying to get at Cravetts, incomprehensible stutterings of outrage and agony bursting from her mouth, streaming tears reddening her empty eyes.

'Shut her up!' Cravetts told his men and turned as the tow-haired Monsher came out of the house shaking his head.

'Where's the other man?' Cravetts said, turning to the woman, across whose mouth Torelli had clamped a grimy fist. She shook her head. Cravetts drew back his hand and hit her across the face with his open palm, flat and hard and mercilessly. Mrs Gibbons' head rocked to one side and a cruel red welt flamed on her cheekbone.

'Talk, damn you!' snarled the raider.

'He's not here,' the woman sobbed. 'Not here.'

'Where, then?'

'He went over to the Fort,' she managed. Then her head came up and the fire came back into her eyes. 'You'll hang for this!' she hissed.

'That'll be the day,' Cravetts said. 'Denny! Milt! Get them horses saddled up. Come on, come on, we don't have all day!'

Three of the raiders were out in the corral, throwing bridles over the heads of the milling horses. Cravetts turned to Torelli.

'Turn her loose,' he said. 'Let her look after her man.'

Torelli nodded and released his hold on Mrs Gibbons and Vister followed suit. Without a second's hesitation the woman went straight for Cravetts' eyes with her hands, her whole body arched with the pent fury of her hatred. Her nails raked a set of tracks down the man's face that went quickly red with bright blood, and Cravetts stood rigid for a moment in utter, astonished rage. Then with a growl that started somewhere deep inside him he grabbed the woman by the arms and threw her away from him. The bodice of her dress tore away in his hands as she went backwards and she fell on her back, her exposed breasts and body startlingly white in the bright sunlight. Cravetts stood for a moment above her, the bright blood staining his collar, his eyes wide with a sudden madness.

And then he fell upon her.

TWO

Frank Angel saw the smoke from a long way off.

He put the spurs to his horse and came over the crest of the bluff going at a flat gallop, heading down towards the burning ranch. He swung off the horse and ran towards the house, shying back from the crackling flames that blasted tangible heat at him.

'Mr Gibbons!' he yelled. 'Dave!'

Nothing moved except the lancing fingers of flame that crept greedily up the charring walls of the house. He ran towards the door and was again beaten back by the flames. He heard the fizzing hiss as his hair singed and then he ran flat out across the yard to the barn. By the door of the barn he saw the dead body of Dave Pugh lying in a sticky pool of blood covered in swarming flies. He ran on past Pugh's body and into the barn, grabbing a horse blanket which he dunked into the horse trough. Wrapping it around his head and shoulders he ran back to the house and charged into the flaming doorway. The big living-room was full of smoke and he began to cough rackingly as it bit into his lungs. He felt the scorching heat of the flames as he breathed and all the oxygen went out of his chest. He stumbled and fell to the floor, and then he saw the bodies in the corner of the room, like a carelessly piled jumble of dirty laundry. The sound of the flames was a constant roar and his eyes were streaming. Lying flat on his belly he scrambled across the floor, steam billowing off the wet blanket. John Gibbons was quite dead; there was a gaping hole in his back where the bullet had exited. He could not tell if Mrs Gibbons was dead or not. Her clothes were torn and her body was bloody but he could not find any wound. He took hold of her feet and started to drag her towards the door. His head was light and he could hear a high whining noise. It took him a minute to realize he was making it himself. The shirt on his back was starting to smoulder and his skin was burning off, he could feel it scorching. Coughing, retching, blind with sticky eyes that no longer could weep, he dragged the woman's body to the door and then across the lintel. Her hair was singed short and blackened at the ends. There were blisters on her skin and he could feel the slippery liquidity of his own burned hands as they touched the bare earth of the yard. He dragged the woman out into the open without quite knowing how he did it; pulling her unceremoniously away from the flames, out into the open.

He managed to get to his feet, his whole body heaving and retching to get oxygen into his lungs, and staggered across to the watering trough, half falling into it. The sudden biting coolness of the water shocked him back into consciousness, and he heard the hiss as the burning wool of his shirt was extinguished. He lay in the blessed chill of the water until his head began to clear and then he got up and tried to walk across to where Stella Gibbons lay. Now he saw her clearly for the first time and realized she was almost naked. He saw the bloody rags of clothing at her crotch and he saw her trying to sit up, her face contorted into a straining mask, the light of pure madness in her eyes as she screamed. Angel's head was light and he thought he must have gone deaf because he could see her stretching her hand towards him and screaming and yet he could hear no sound coming from her. Yet he could hear the terrible crackling of the burning house and then he knew what had happened and as he realized it he started to run towards her and halfway there he slipped straight down into unconsciousness and crumpled in a heap upon the ground.

'He's coming round.'

No I'm not, Angel thought petulantly. *No I'm not.*

But he came on up out of the darkness and felt the pain for the first time, alive and pure white and just below the threshold of unbearability all over his body: his back, his shoulders, arms and hands. He opened his eyes. A bed. He moved his head right and left. Beds. A hospital. Then it all came back and he knew where he was and he lifted his head to look at the Army uniforms, the Post Surgeon standing at the end of the bed, the orderly with the medical chart in his hands taking notes.

'How are you feeling, young man?' the doctor asked.

'All right, I guess,' Angel said. Then he remembered more and said 'Mrs Gibbons! Is she—'

The Army man shook his head.

'You've been out for two days, son. Mrs Gibbons died the night we brought her in here.'

Angel shook his head. The memory would not go away: the straining face, the empty eyes, that soundless, awful scream. . . .

'Did she—' He stopped himself. There was no way she could have talked.

He tried again.

'Did you find out what happened?'

The Army doctor nodded. 'Mrs Gibbons tried to write a little of it down. We were able to piece it together from what we found out there.'

14

'How did you—'

'Son, people in this country see smoke they know it's trouble,' the doctor said. 'Al Woodward damn' near killed a team of horses getting to the Gibbons place. Found you and the woman lying in the yard more dead than alive, and got you over here as fast as he could travel. You owe him your life: if you'd lain out there much longer you'd have died from exposure.'

'How badly am I hurt?' Angel asked.

'Some bad burning on your back,' the doctor said. 'Nothing too serious. How old are you, son?'

'Twenty,' Angel said. 'Why?'

'You're young,' the soldier replied. 'Your skin will heal fast. We'll have you up and about in a week or so.'

'A week or so!' burst out Angel. 'I want to be out of here faster than that. Whoever burned the ranch—'

'We know who they were, boy. I told you, Mrs Gibbons tried to write down what she could. We've got patrols out now scouring the country for them. Don't worry, they'll not get far.'

'You want to tell me what happened?' Angel said.

The doctor nodded. 'Don't see why not. After what you did back there, I reckon you deserve that, if we can't get you a medal.'

'Skip the medal,' Angel said.

The Army surgeon nodded. Then he outlined the meagre facts that they had been able to get from Stella Gibbons before she died. She had named the men as well as she could from memory. Told how they killed her husband and Dave Pugh. Then what they had done to her.

'Savages!' ground out the doctor. 'If it was Indians, I could understand it. But white men!'

'They slit her tongue?'

'To stop her screaming while they raped her, I

15

suppose,' said the doctor.

'Then they set fire to the house and just tossed her in to burn alive.' He shook his head again, pounding a fist into his palm. 'Savages!'

'They were after the horses?'

'That's our reading of it, son. They left behind some pretty brokendown animals – probably stolen, too. If we can get a line on them, we may know more about the men who stole them. All we got right now is some names, and we're not altogether sure how accurate they are.'

'I want you to write them down for me,' Angel said.

'Sure, I – what for?' the doctor checked himself. 'If you've got any ideas of going after those men—'

'Just get me the names,' Angel said.

'No way,' replied the soldier. 'The Army will handle this.'

'Sure,' Angel said. 'When can I get up?'

'Let's wait a few more days and see, shall we?' said the doctor, cheerfully. 'You've got to get some strength back into your legs first. Now take a sip of this.' He poured some liquid into a cup and added water. It had a violet colour.

'What's that?' Angel said.

'Just drink it,' urged the doctor, watching as Angel gulped it down. He nodded. 'Good,' he said, and pulled his watch from his fob pocket, watching Angel as he did so. Angel felt an undertow of tiredness. It was like mist coming up from the river bottoms on a November night. Each time you shifted your eyes, it seemed to have come closer without moving at all. He looked at the doctor, who was smiling.

'You bastard,' Angel said, and slid down into sleep as the doctor put the laudanum back into his bag. He beckoned the orderly across.

'He'll be out until about noon tomorrow,' he said.

16

'When he comes to, don't talk with him about – what happened.'

'Yessir,' said the orderly, wondering if the doctor would ever get the message that running the Post Hospital and tending to the patients and acting as assistant vet was a full time job and if anyone thought he had time to stand around chattering with fresh-faced farm kids who wouldn't know their asses from holes in the ground then he had another think coming.

After a week, Frank Angel was fit enough to ride.

He thanked the doctor for his care, and the old man grinned the thanks away.

'I trust you've gotten over that stupid idea you had of going after those bandits,' he said. Angel nodded.

'Hell, yes,' he said. 'What could I do, anyway? I don't even own a gun.'

'That's the sensible way to look at it, son,' the doctor assured him. 'They're bad medicine. The way we have it, they robbed the Paymaster at Fort Riley, killed five men doing it. Them horses we found at the Gibbons place were stolen from up Zanedale way. So they're not only on the run from the local law, they're on the run from the United States Army and the Department of Justice as well.'

'Department of Justice?' Angel asked, raising his eyebrows.

'Sure, son, the Justice Department is responsible for the prosecution of all cases involving the breaking of Federal law. Robbing an Army payroll is a Federal offence. Those fellows have got every lawman in the country on their tails.'

'They'll be long gone out of Kansas now,' Angel said, reflectively. 'New Mexico, maybe, or Arizona. Who knows?'

'Don't you fret, boy. They'll be caught. And hanged. John Gibbons was too good a man.'

'I know,' Angel said, quietly. 'He was the nearest thing to a father I ever had.'

The doctor nodded, then harrumphed.

'What are you going to do now, may I ask?'

Angel shook his head. 'Find me another job some- place,' he said. 'There's plenty of work around. Railroad'll be coming through in another year or two.'

'Well,' said the doctor. 'Well. If there's anything I—'

'Thanks, doc, you already did plenty,' Angel smiled. He extended his hand and the gruff old Army man shook it.

'Come back and see me anytime,' he said, 'as long as it's on your own two feet!' Then, almost abruptly, he turned and marched away, his spine erect and soldierly as he crossed the parade ground and went into the offi- cers' quarters on the west side of the Fort.

Frank Angel led his horse up the street to the sutler's store and went inside. He found Al Woodward sitting at a table, a drink of beer in front of him.

'Mr Woodward,' Angel said. 'I wanted to thank you.'

'You're damned welcome, boy,' Woodward said. 'Glad I was able to help out.' He shook his head. 'Those filthy bastards!'

'It must have been pretty bad for you, bringing Mrs Gibbons in the way you did,' Angel said quietly. 'I wish I could have done it.'

'You did more than enough, boy,' Woodward said. 'But I'd sure like to get my hands on that Cravetts jasper. I'd tie knots in his stinking neck!'

'Cravetts?' Angel said.

'Yeah, sure,' Woodward said. 'He's the one Stella – Mrs Gibbons – said was in charge of them bravos.'

'I never heard the name before,' Angel said. 'How

come they'd pick on the Gibbons place?'

'Beats me, son,' Woodward said. 'Way I figger her, they stopped someplace an' asked the whereabouts of a horse ranch. Someone told 'em that Gibbons raised hosses, an' that was that.'

'Cravetts,' repeated Angel. 'Did she – Mrs Gibbons – give any idea what he looked like?'

'I don't know, Frank,' Woodward said. 'The so'jer boys took all the notes. I just heard some scuttlebutt in the store, here.'

'What else?' Angel insisted.

'Nothin' really,' Woodward said. 'Couple o' names. That Cravetts. Feller named Monsher what had tow-hair an' a Southern accent. An' some Eye-talian name like Barelli, Tiratti, somethin' like that.' He swung to face the younger man, his eyes bleary with the beer. 'You wanna beer?' he asked. Angel shook his head. Woodward got lumberingly to his feet and said 'I got to get another beer. Keep seein' that girl's face. . . .' He shook his head.

'Mr Woodward, I got to be going,' Frank Angel said.

'Sure, boy,' Woodward said, and lurched off to the counter. Frank Angel went out into the bright sunlight and stood there for a long minute, watching the busy formalities of the military post. Fort Dodge was still quite a new fort; when he had come out to this part of the country in '66, they were still finishing it off.

Frank Angel took stock of himself. He had a horse and saddle. He had a set of hand-me-down clothes that had been found for him on the Fort. He had some money – a few dollars, no more. And three names.

It was enough to make a start on.

He climbed into the saddle and pointed the pony north.

That night he was in Fort Larned.

THREE

It took him nearly three weeks.

During that time he worked as a teamster for the military at Fort Larned – some of the older soldiers still called it Camp Alert, the name the post had been given before the War between the States. They gave him a bed in the loft above the sutler's store, a big sandstone building with a Dutch barn roof that stood on the edge of the perimeter, right-angled to the line of officers' quarters. Larned was a big establishment, bustling day and night with activity as the soldiers moved in and out on patrol, and civilians came and went with supplies. Over the weeks, Angel met most of the local farmers and ranchers, and always asked them the same question. About three men looking for a horse ranch.

They would shake their heads, scratch their ears, screw up their eyes reflectively. They would go back to their wagons sometimes and ask their womenfolk. Kids would come around and chant nursery rhymes as he waited outside ranch houses where he was making some kind of delivery, and he would ask hired hands, cowboys he met on the open country. Nobody remembered them.

Then the third week, he got a break.

He was hauling some Michigan pine that had been shipped in by rail as far as Kansas City and then teamed down the Santa Fé Trail to Fort Dodge. He picked it up at the depot and headed on north up towards the Heimberger place on Buckner Creek.

Heimberger was a sharp-featured, blond-haired man of about forty, well built and burned dark brown from the years he had spent in the open. He had three sons and the five of them made pretty short work of unloading the pine, which Heimberger was using to build an extra room on to his three-room shack.

'Is getting rather zmall,' he said, 'for us so a lot'

'Erwin!' called his wife. 'You bring that young man inside for some lemonade when you're finished out there, y'hear?'

'That wife of mine,' Heimberger smiled, shaking his head. 'Fifteen years we are married together, still she calls me like a zmall boy.'

Angel grinned. He reckoned the rancher didn't mind it all that much. They trooped into the house, welcoming the shade after the hard heat of the open yard. Mrs Heimberger was a slender woman, as blonde as her husband, with a face just short of prettiness. She asked Angel where he was from and he told her,

'You worked for Chon Gibbons?' Heimberger asked, his eyebrows going up. ''Ve heard at the Fort about what happened there. It was you who. . . ?'

'Yessir, it was me,' Angel replied. 'I got to be getting along.'

He had had a lot of that. When he asked his questions they always put it together and then they wanted to know the details. He did not think he would ever tell anyone the details.

'I feel very . . . very . . .' Heimberger snapped his fingers in exasperation when the word would not come.

'Guilty, you mean?' his wife supplied.

'*Ja, gültig* – guilty,' he said. 'I think I sent those men there.' He looked up into Frank Angel's eyes and fell

21

back from the blazing light in them. His own eyes widened, and flickered nervously towards the rifle hanging over the mantelpiece.

'I know nothing of them then,' he said, holding up a hand as though to ward off a psychic attack. Angel sat motionless in the chair, his eyes fixed on the German.

'We had some men come by the house asking for directions to a horse ranch,' Mrs Heimberger explained. 'We took no real notice of it then. Only afterwards: we wondered. That was all, we just wondered.'

'Did they give you any names?' Frank Angel asked.

Heimberger shook his head.

'No,' he said. 'They were chust riding through. They did not stop, even, for coffee.'

'Can you recall what any of them looked like?' Angel persisted.

Heimberger frowned. Then his frown lifted and his face brightened.

'*Ja*, I can remember somethings. That one who talked – you remember it, *schatz*, the one with the shoulders so.'

'Oh, yes,' Mrs Heimberger said. 'The leader – at least I'd reckon he was. He was a big man across. Big chested, heavy set. Black hair and a beard coming along. Very soft spoken, he was.'

'Cravetts,' Angel said.

'What is that Cravats?' Heimberger said.

'That was his name,' the younger man replied. 'Cravetts.'

'You know their names?'

'Three of them. Cravetts. Monsher. And one with an Italian-sounding name. Barelli, or Tiratti.'

'But the soldiers . . .' Heimbreger said.

'Sure, they know,' Angel replied. 'But they aren't about to tell me. Army business, they say.'

'But you are thinking not,' Heimberger probed.

'I am thinking not,' Angel said.

'They were hard ones,' the rancher pointed out. 'Not ordinary ranch hands. Thieves. Guerillas, perhaps, from the War days. You were in the War?'

'In a way,' Angel said. He did not elaborate.

'Seven of them,' Mrs Heimberger said. 'I remember thinking, John Gibbons would be pleased if he could sell seven horses.'

'Can you remember anything else about them?' pleaded the younger man. 'Anything at all?'

'Well . . .' The woman frowned, throwing her thoughts back. 'It was late in the afternoon. None of them spoke, you see. Only the leader – Cravetts, you said his name was?' Angel nodded. 'There was one with glasses, I remember that. Wait, now. He called him something. Denny! That was it. Denny, the one with glasses. Short, a bit on the flabby side. With glasses. Thick lips. Denny.'

'Denny,' Angel said. 'Is that all you can remember?'

'I'm sorry,' she said. 'They really didn't say much, you see.'

'We would help more if we could,' her husband added.

'Pa,' one of the boys said. The rancher held up his hand. His sons had been listening to the whole conversation spellbound. When the eldest one spoke, his father made the standard parental 'don't interrupt' sign. 'But Pa,' the boy said.

'Not now, Chris,' he said.

'They said they hadn't had a drink since Abilene, Pa, I heard them!' burst out the boy. 'The one with the squinty eyes.'

Angel swung around to face the boy.

'Tell me,' he said.

'I was in the barn, over behind them,' Chris said. 'I

23

heard them a-talkin', the one with the squinty eyes and the redhaired one.'

'You have not said about this before to me,' Heimberger growled.

'We never done talked none about it, Pa,' Chris said.

'Talk now,' Heimberger commanded. 'Tell it all.'

'Well, like I said, I was in the barn. Steve and Paul was milkin', an' I heard them fellers ride up. I sorta sneaked behind the door an' watched. This squinty-eyed one, on the sorrel, he was talkin' to the red-headed one like I told you. The red-headed one says "I sure could use a drink," and the squinty-eyed one says "Yeah, Dick sure is pushin' us along. We ain't had a drink since Abilene".'

'He used the name Dick?' Angel said. 'That would be the boss?'

'Guess so,' the youngster said.

'Anything else?'

'Well, nothin' much, really. . . .' the boy fidgeted.

'You can say it,' Heimberger said.

'Uh . . . well . . .'

'They was talkin' 'bout women,' interjected the youngest of the trio, Paul. He was about eight. 'Chris told Steve an' I heard him!'

'Paul, I'll larrup you!' shouted Chris, his face crimson.

'Is too late arguing,' Heimberger said '*Mutti*, better now you leave us a moment.'

'Erwin Heimberger, if you think . . .' Her lips set in a firm thin line as she saw her husband's head dip, bull-like. 'Very well!' She marched into her kitchen and they heard the furious rattle of pans.

'Better now you tell me everything,' Heimberger said.

'He said – the squinty-eyed one – he said he was gettin' horny.'

'Horny? What is this horny?'

'You know, Pa, like the bull,' little Paul supplied helpfully. Heimberger eyed his youngest son balefully. The boy shrank back behind his older brother, lips trembling halfway between fear and laughter.

'Go on,' Angel prompted. 'It's OK.'

'The red-headed one said "Milt, if you're horny after all the pussy you had in Abilene, I swear to God they ain't never goin' to make enough." I didn't understand that bit, but then the squinty-eyed one said "Little Rosie sure could love a man". I knew what he meant then.'

'He called the man with the squint Milt?'

'That's right, mister.'

'You hear anything else? Any other names? Anything at all?'

'No sir, that's all I heard, honest.'

'Enough, I think,' Heimberger said, heavily. But there was a light in his eyes and the boys could read it and they grinned. Angel felt the tug of their affection for each other. It made him lonely for a moment. Then he got up from the table and drained the lemonade glass.

'Mr Heimberger, I don't know how I'm going to thank you and your family. But I thank you.'

'That is nothing,' Heimberger said. 'You will tell all this to the Army people?'

'I expect so,' Angel said non-committally. 'I better be moving on.'

They came to the door and stood there together as he swung aboard the wagon and gigged the horses into movement. When he was a long way from the house he looked back. He thought he could see them all standing in the yard waving. He turned round and set his face towards the empty land.

By nightfall he was back at Fort Larned. Next day he told the teamster boss he was quitting and drew his pay. It was the most money he had ever had in his life.

He went into the post trader's store and waited until

the proprietor finished serving a sergeant who was buying some twine.

'Howdy, son,' the storekeeper said. 'What can I do for you?'

He was a swarthy man, with a walrus moustache and liquid brown eyes. A cigarette dangled from his lips.

'I want to buy a gun,' Frank Angel said. 'What can I get for twenty dollars?'

The man looked at him for a moment, squinting through the cigarette smoke. Then he laughed, a short sound like a dog barking.

'Damn all, I'd say,' he said. 'Damn all.'

'Haven't you got anything?' Angel asked. 'It doesn't have to be new.'

'You're meanin' a handgun, I reckon?' the storekeeper said.

Frank Angel nodded. 'How much is a sixgun?'

The storekeeper made his barking noise again. 'More'n you got, sonny,' he said. 'More'n you got.'

The younger man's face set. 'You want to sell me a gun or don't you?' he snapped. 'This isn't the only trading post in Kansas.'

The storekeeper raised his arms in mock alarm. 'Hey, easy there, pardner,' he said wheezily. 'I was just havin' a little fun.'

'We'll say you've had it,' Angel said. 'Now: you got a gun or not?'

'Wait a minnit,' the man said. He went into the store-room in back of the building, and Angel heard him rummaging about in there, wheezing, coughing regularly. After about five minutes the man came out. He had a wooden box in his hands and he opened it and laid it on the counter.

'There's this,' he offered. 'Needs a little attention, here an' there. But it's a nice handgun.'

Angel lifted the gun out of the box, where it lay wrapped in an oil-damp rag. It was an 1860 .44 Army Colt. One of the wooden grips on the butt was badly cracked and loose to the touch. The 8" barrel was pitted a little, but not badly. Angel tried the hammer, which slicked back smoothly, and checking the sights – the nock in the top of the hammer and the foresight – he found them well-aligned. The gun had been hard-used but not ruined. He pushed out the retaining lug and let the chamber slip into his hand, then squinted up the barrel. It looked clean and unscarred.

'Fair,' he said.

'You're an expert,' the storekeeper said. There was deep sarcasm in his voice. Angel ignored it.

'How much?'

'Twenty dollars,' the man said.

'You throw in some powder an' caps, some tools and moulds, and a holster, you've got a deal,' Angel said.

'Maybe you'd like a horse as well,' said the store-keeper. 'What you think this is, some kind o' charity organization?'

'I think it's a place where a crook like you would try to sell a ten dollar gun to a kid he thought didn't know any better,' Frank Angel said flatly. 'Am I right?'

'Now, see here . . .' blustered the man. 'I got half a mind . . .'

'An' it shows,' Angel snapped. 'Stop trying to run a sandy on me, mister. Get the rest of the stuff or take your damned gun and shove it up your ass.' He banged the revolver down on the counter and the storekeeper jumped. There was something in the cold eyes of this youngster that made him nervous about pushing his sarcasm one step further. A man who ran a store this far west saw a lot of hardcases, young and old, and learned one thing if nothing else. Sell them what they wanted

27

and get them out of the place as fast as possible. He proceeded to do just that and Angel left ten minutes later with the Army Colt strapped to his hip in a flap-top cavalry holster. The cartridge cases and powder he put into his saddle-bags together with the flask and the bullet mould. The percussion caps he slipped into a shirt pocket. Then he went to get his horse from the stable on the southern edge of the rectangle made by the Fort. He looked around Larned one last time as he mounted up: the sandstone buildings with their white-framed windows, the neat-porched officers' quarters, the slender flagpole in the centre of the square, the rows of saplings clinging desperately to life in the relentless sun. He put the river on his right and turned the horse towards the Great Bend. Three days later he was in Abilene.

FOUR

He came out of the Alamo saloon on Texas Street.

He had a frock coat and a low-crowned hat with a wide brim. His hair was long and corn-yellow in the sunlight, hanging down to his shoulders. He leaned up against the wall of the saloon and hooked his thumbs into the red sash that encircled his waist and Angel saw that he had two ivory-handled sixguns stuck into the sash, butts facing inwards towards each other. The man watched everything that moved on the street and the sidewalks from under his eyebrows. There was plenty to watch on Texas Street.

The sidewalks were crowded with people. Bunches of cowboys up from Texas with the herds careened in and out of the saloons, yelling and yipping, lurching drunkenly, catcalling to the whores parading up and down in their white-tasselled half boots and cheap finery. Wagons lurched up and down the street, their drivers cursing the mules. Children played here and there in the dust, or ran shouting, in and out and around the lumbering traffic. Horses stood hipshot outside the saloons: the Bull's Head and the Alamo and the Longhorn. Angel caught a whiff of burning grease from a lunch wagon parked at the sidewalk near the Longhorn. Men stood in front of it or were hunkered down on the sidewalk, scooping food from tin plates, and oblivious of the murderous looks of businessmen who had to step around them on their way to the post office or the First National Bank of Kansas City. A piano player was belting out a tune in the Longhorn and now and then hoarse shouts erupted from the place. The man leaning against the wall of the Alamo saloon watched everything and remained motionless. Angel crossed the street towards him. He saw the pale blue eyes touch him and then move away, then come back again as he kept on coming. Without any haste, the tall man eased his back off the wall. His hands stayed hooked in the red sash. When Angel got within ten feet of him, the man spoke.

'You want something?' he said. His eyes were on the gun at Angel's side.

'Like to ask you something, Mr Hickok,' Angel said.

'Ask away,' Hickok said.

'I'm looking for some men who were here about six weeks ago. Seven men.'

'Lot of men come through here, sonny,' Hickok said. His voice had a nasal, Eastern drone.

'Yessir, I know,' Angel said. 'I just figured, you being the Marshal, you might have run across them.'

'Come on inside and you can buy me a drink,' Hickok said. 'Glad to help if I can.'

He stood courteously on one side to allow Frank Angel to precede him into the noisy saloon. The place was jumping. Men were two and three deep at the long bar, drinking as if someone had served notice of a forthcoming drought. Keno, chuckaluck, faro layouts were roaring. There were men everywhere playing cards. Girls circulated around the tables, stroking necks and touching thighs, smiling invitingly. The air was thick with tobacco smoke and smelled like a barn.

'Over here,' Hickok said.

There was a table in a blind corner of the room. It had three chairs around it: one in the angle of the two walls, the other two facing. Hickok sat in the angle of the walls, lifting his coat so that it fell away to the sides. The gun butts rapped the table.

'My private table,' he explained. He lifted a hand, and one of the girls nodded and came over.

'Belle, bring us something to drink,' he said.

'Sure, Bill,' the girl said, smiling widely. Her face was painted like a doll's and she reeked of cheap perfume. Hickok patted her buttocks and she winked and twitched her hips saucily. Her eyes were as empty as a hollow tree.

'What's your handle, son?' Hickok asked.

'Angel, sir,' Angel replied. 'Frank Angel.'

Hickok smiled. 'You get teased much about it?'

'Not since I got my full growth,' the boy replied.

'And you're looking for some men,' Hickok prompted, pouring two sizable drinks from the bottle the girl Belle brought, still simpering at the marshal.

'Seven men,' Angel told him. 'I only got a rough description and some names. Cravetts was their leader. Thickset, very wide across the shoulders, black hair and starting a beard. A tow-haired one with a Southern accent named Monsher. A squint-eyed man called Milt, and another with red hair. One of the others was called Denny. Wore glasses. Two others. I don't know anything about them except one of them had an Italian-sounding name.'

Hickok pursed his lips. 'Riding together, you say?'

'Far as I know.'

'I don't recall seeing them,' Hickok said. Angel's face fell, and the lawman smiled. 'That don't mean shucks, boy. If they didn't make any trouble here, I'd have no reason to remember them at all.'

'I know it,' Angel said. 'It was a long shot at the best.

Thanks anyway.' He put a dollar on the table for the drinks and rose to go. Hickok rose too, and Angel noticed again that the slim hands were not too far away from the ivory-handled guns.

'You got any idea where I could find a girl called Rosie, or Little Rosie?' Angel asked.

Hickok laughed. 'Son, there's about a thousand girls in McCoy's Addition,' he smiled. 'Any one o' them could be called Rosie an' probably is.'

Angel nodded. Then: 'Could you – maybe, ask your – uh, friend?'

Hickok laughed again, and heads turned towards him. Angel noticed that many of the faces were hostile. Hickok was obviously not popular among the cowboy element. He'd read one or two things about Abilene in the newspapers which came infrequently his way on the Gibbons ranch and at the Fort. Hickok was said to be terrifyingly fast with his guns, and a born killer. Yet here he seemed the soul of courtesy, and apart from his florid style of dress, a gentleman.

'Belle!' Hickok called, and the girl came mincing over. 'My young friend here is looking for a girl named Rosie.'

Belle eyed the younger man speculatively and let a pink tongue slide provocatively across her rouged lips.

'Oh, come on, cowboy,' she said, slipping an arm through Angel's, 'you'll have a much better time with Belle, won't he Bill?'

'You'd eat him for breakfast,' Hickok grinned. 'Leave off, and answer the question.'

'Rosie, Rosie, Rosie,' Belle said. 'Rosie Russell, mebbe? She works over to the Longhorn. There's Rosie something-or-other has a place back up in the Addition. Hell, Bill, there's mebbe half a dozen. Who can keep track of all of them? They come out here like flies.'

'Looks like you're going to have to do it the hard way, son,' Hickok said, as the girl flounced off again. 'Ploddin' around an' askin'.' Angel nodded. 'I guess so,' he said.

'You got much money, boy?' Hickok asked abruptly.

'No sir, not much,' Frank Angel admitted. Hickok nodded. 'Can you use that thing?' he gestured with his chin towards Angel's gun.

'Uh . . . I . . . yes, I can shoot a bit.'

'That means you can't. Take it off.'

'What?' Frank Angel looked at the Marshal in surprise. 'Take it off an' give it to me,' Hickok said.

Frank Angel was suddenly aware that the entire saloon had frozen, and everyone had stopped speaking simultaneously as Hickok gave the order. Chairs scraped nervously as men tried to edge out of line of possible fire behind Angel. Hickok just kept on looking at the younger man and Angel shrugged. He unbuckled the belt and holster and laid them on the table. Immediately the chatter and the noise began again, and Hickok smiled.

'You go poking your nose around the Addition totin' a gun, someone's just liable to invite you to use it for the hell of it. You know how folks are about questions in these parts.'

'I know,' Angel said, 'I'm going to ask just the same.'

'You take care, boy,' Hickok said. 'On'y go down there in the daytime.'

'I'll do that, Mr Hickok,' Angel said. 'I guess you're right about the gun.'

'About guns I'm always right, son,' Hickok said. 'I'll walk to the door with you.' He went ahead of Angel and pushed the batwings wide, scanning the street carefully before he stepped out on to the sidewalk. Only then did Frank Angel realize he had shielded Hickok's back the entire way with his own body. He shook his head. Why would a man want to stay in a job where he had to do that every day of his life?

Hickok saw the head-shake and smiled.

'Plenty o' men in this town who'd like to see me dead, boy,' he said. 'More who'd like to go back to Texas with a notch on their sixgun for Wild Bill. I take as few chances as I can, draw my hundred an' fifty a month, an' keep the town as quiet as possible.'

Angel gestured with his chin at the crowded, brawling, rowdy street. 'That's quiet?' he asked.

'You wait until Saturday night,' Hickok said. He settled his back comfortably against the wooden wall of the saloon and tipped his hat slightly forward. 'Pick up your hogleg before you leave town,' he said, and that was the end of the interview. Angel saw he was dismissed from the gunfighter's mind. Hickok's eyes were already monitoring everything moving on the street once more.

He headed down Texas Street towards the Longhorn and went in. It was as crowded and noisy and smoky as the Alamo had been, and he had to literally force a way through the crowd packed at the bar to ask the bartender a question.

The bartender looked up and scanned the seething room with a practised eye. 'Over there with the big cowboy,' he said. 'Gal with the red dress on. Listen, wait . . .' he tried to restrain Angel but it was too late, and the bartender shrugged. He tapped one of the barflies on the shoulder and whispered something to him and the man nodded quickly and went out through the batwings fast as Angel crossed the room towards the table where the girl in the red dress was sitting. A tall, black-haired cowboy was pawing her clumsily and she was giggling. Angel pushed through until he was standing close to the table.

'Excuse me,' he said.

The cowboy looked up. He was drunk and his eyes were already smoky with sexual anticipation. 'Piss off,' he growled.

'I just wanted to ask . . .'

'You heard!' snapped the cowboy. 'Get out o' here.'

Angel ignored him. 'Your name Rosie?' he asked. 'Rosie Russell?' The girl looked up and simpered. 'What if it is?' she said.

'Like to ask you a few questions,' Angel said. 'About some men . . .'

The cowboy came up away from his chair in a lurching movement and leaned forward on the table. His was two or three inches taller than Angel's almost six foot height, and his eyes were glowing now with a liquor-hazed rage.

'Sonny, you want your ass broke ?' he yelled.

'No, sir,' Angel said.

'Then get the hell out o' here afore I break it for you!' growled the cowboy. The girl pouted. Everyone in the place was watching the exchange, ready for a fast dive out of range if trouble broke.

'Aw, c'mon, honey,' she said to the cowboy. 'He ain't doin' no harm. He's only a kid.'

'You shut up an' sit down here,' the cowboy said. 'An' you do like I told you, boy!'

He pushed the girl into her chair, and she gasped, the breath jarred out of her by his roughness.

'That's awful rude of you,' Angel said mildly. He took two smooth steps around the table and hit the cowboy solidly in the middle. The man looked at him with bulging eyes, the breath whooshing out of his lungs as he folded forward on the table. The chair went over backwards away from him and the girl screamed. Men pushed back away from the area as fast as they could, getting to their feet and yelling as the big cowboy got his breath and then with a roar of rage came over the table at the slim youngster in front of him. Angel let him come and then hit him, a short lifting hook made with the hand tipped backwards. The heel of his hand caught the cowboy right under the jaw and snapped his head back, mashing the snarling lips into a blood-sprayed mask. He went sideways across the table, tipping it over to the filthy, packed-dirt floor. A roar of animal rage escaped his broken mouth, and he started to come up from the floor. Angel let him get up off his knees before he moved again and then he linked both his hands together and swung them from right to left, just as if he was holding an axe in them. It was an awful blow and it hit the cowboy on the side of his face where the jawbone hinges in front of the ear. Everyone in the place heard the bone go, and the cowboy screamed in agony, the side of his face suddenly slack and old. He went down squirming in the wreckage of the table and Angel stood watching him. Every trace of boyishness was gone from his stance and the eyes were empty and cold. No one moved for a moment, then Angel turned and spoke.

'It's over,' he said. His chest was splattered with the cowboy's blood.

'No it ain't, sonny!' someone snarled.

Angel whirled around.

There was a Texas cowboy near the bar, his hand curled above the butt of a sixshooter nestling low on his right hip in a cutaway holster.

'You got five seconds to say a prayer, pilgrim,' the cowboy said, 'And then I'm gonna shoot your balls off!'

FIVE

'Don't touch that gun, cowboy!'

Every head in the place turned towards the voice. Many of them knew its nasal tone already, and those who did not certainly knew its owner. Hickok stood in the doorway, his hands hooked in the red sash, his forearms holding back the opened frock coat. The ivory-handled Colts were ready, jutting forward.

'Hickok, this ain't none o' your say-so!' the cowboy said. 'This is atween me an' the kid here!'

'I'd normally say you were right,' Hickok said, his voice level and unruffled. 'However, I happen to know the boy isn't heeled. Which would make shootin' him murder, which in turn would make it some o' my say-so. Now: you still anxious to pull that iron?'

His eyes narrowed slightly, and he braced his feet slightly apart. For a long, long moment the cowboy glared at him, his hand poised near the cutaway holster. Then, with an oath, he turned away and put both hands palm down on the bar. Hickok nodded, and came into the saloon, easing neatly along the bar with his back to it until he came level with the cowboy. He lifted the man's gun from the holster and tossed it to a shorter, thickset man near the door who wore a badge.

'Take him along, Mike,' he said.

The deputy nodded and gestured with the man's gun, which he cocked ostentatiously. Hickok eeled back towards the door using that curious motion which precluded anyone's getting around in back of him. He pushed the cowboy in front of him.

'Don't shove me, dammit!' snarled the cowboy. 'I ain't no whore you can hustle!'

There was a quick sound of indrawn breath as the man uttered the words. It was one thing to call a man like Hickok a pimp behind his back, quite another to do it to his face. Hickok's face went white.

'You want to back that up, outside?' he hissed.

'I ain't goin' up against you, Hickok!' the cowboy shouted. 'One o' these days us Texicans'll get together an' wipe you out!'

'But not today,' Hickok said quietly. Nobody saw his hands move yet suddenly there was a flash of light as he drew one of the ivory-handled sixguns and whipped it alongside the cowboy's head. The man fell as if poleaxed; and Hickok whirled in one fluid movement to face the crowded room.

'Any more o' you Texicans want in on this?' he said. He used the word Texicans like some foul insult.

Nobody moved.

Hickok nodded, and then said to Angel, who was still standing by the wrecked table, 'You better get out o' here, sonny.'

'When I'm through,' Angel said doggedly.

Hickok smiled. 'Come see me,' he said, and then gestured brusquely at some of the bystanders. They lifted the two fallen Texans roughly and carted them out through the doors. When they had gone a clamour of shouts for drinks, some ribald shouts and jeers broke loose. No one came near Angel, who sat down in the chair next to the saloon girl and pulled it close to her.

She looked at him with wide eyes.

'You're a right one, aren't you?' she said, coyly.

'Ma'am?'

'You don't look much more than a baby,' she cooed. 'Yet you're . . .' she leaned over and squeezed his biceps. 'Oooh,' she said.

'Listen,' Angel said. 'I want to ask you about a man called Milt.'

'Oooh, ducky,' she giggled. 'You don't look the type.'

A bottle and glass was plonked on the table by a passing waiter.

'I don't—' Angel began.

'—you got to buy me a drink, dearie,' the girl said. 'House rules.'

He shrugged and she poured him a sizable slug of whiskey. He felt her hand go to his groin and in spite of himself he was aroused. He pushed her away.

'Go on,' she said. 'You know you like it.'

'Business first,' he said, forcing a leer. 'Fun later.'

'Oooh,' she said again, 'you're a right one, you are.'

'Your name Rosie Russell?' Angel asked.

'That's right, dearie. Me professional name,' she said, flirting her curls. Her face looked pathetically young beneath the heavy mask of powder and paint.

'You know a man called Milt?' he asked. 'Rode through here maybe five, six weeks back, with six other guys?'

The girl put her head back and laughed aloud, a caterwauling gurgle that had no mirth in it whatsoever.

'We see a thousand cowboys a month in Abilene, dearie,' she laughed. 'Who can remember every one that buys a girl a drink?'

'He bought more than a drink, Rosie,' Angel said. 'He bought you a hell of a good time. I'd have thought you remembered anyone who did that.'

'Depends,' she said, pouting. 'You surely ain't doin' much.'

'I only got ten dollars,' he lied. 'If you come up with what I want to know, it's yours.'

The girl's eyes went instantly calculating. Ten dollars was not a lot of money but it was better than doing five tricks.

'You're a queer duck an' no mistake,' she sighed, nestling her head against him. Her hand moved urgently beneath the table. 'Why don't we go into one of the side booths an'. . . talk?'

Angel reached into his vest pocket and pulled out a pouch. He emptied it on the table: ten silver dollars.

'Take it,' he said. 'Then you'll quit trying to get me into a deadfall. Rosie, you're a pretty girl and I like you, but I got to find this Milt fellow.'

'I can keep the money?' she asked. 'No kidding?' The way she said it touched him: nobody could have ever given her a truthful answer to that question.

'Keep it,' he said, pushing the money towards her. 'Tell me about Milt.'

'Nothin' much to tell, really,' she said, deftly sweeping the money into the pouch and stuffing it down between her breasts. 'Him and his friend Howard.'

'Howard? Did he have red hair?'

'That's right, how did you know?' When Angel didn't answer, she went on, 'Anyways, they came in one night and this Milt made a big fuss of me, buyin' champagne, orderin' the best room in the place. We had quite a night of it all.'

'You and Milt and Howard?'

'Plus another friend of mine, an older lady who acted as our chaperone,' Rosie said, demurely.

'Did they say anything at all about themselves, Rosie? Think,' he urged her, 'it's very important.'

'No,' she said. 'No, I'd remember if they had. They were heading south,' she giggled. 'But they wasn't in no hurry.' A wary look crossed her face. 'What you asking all these questions for?'

'I have to find Milt,' he lied. 'His folks an' mine are neighbours back in Missouri. His old man is awful sick and he asked me to see if I could track him down and get him to head back for Kearney.'

'Oh, that poor man,' she said. 'His daddy must be pretty old, I reckon.' Angel said nothing, and she went on, 'Milt bein' thirty five, I mean.'

'He's seventy two,' Angel said, doing some quick arithmetic.

'Poor Mr Sharp,' the girl said. She was silent for a moment, and Angel started to rise. 'No, wait,' the girl said. 'I'll tell you. I just remembered something, about where Milt said they were heading.'

'Tell me,' Angel said.

'You're hurting my arm,' she pointed out mildly. He loosened his grip. 'Milt said something about not seeing another woman this side of the Raton Pass.'

'He said that – Raton Pass?'

She nodded. 'They was heading for New Mexico. But I don't know where – hey!' She slapped her leg and turned to a man sitting next to her at the next table.

'How do you like that – he never even said goodbye!'

'Never mind, sis,' the man grinned. He was a bushy-haired fellow of perhaps thirty, with the weatherbeaten face of an outdoorsman. 'You'll do better talkin' to me, anyways.' He put an arm round her waist and lifted her up, plonking her down on his lap. She wriggled a little and her cheeks flushed slightly.

'Oooh,' she said, 'you're a right one, aren't you. What's your name, dearie?'

'Dick,' he said.

The girl's high-pitched giggle cut through the hubbub of the room and one or two heads turned. Otherwise nobody took any notice at all. No more notice was taken of Frank Angel as he pushed through the batwings and headed up Texas Street towards the marshal's office on the corner. It was a makeshift affair of log, the gaps between the pine horizontals slapped carelessly with white gypsum cement, the dried bark peeling everywhere. The door was sturdy and heavy, with no windows. Inside there was a long room with a desk in the corner – again, a blind corner with no windows, Angel noticed. Behind it and across the room floor-to-ceiling bars separated another area that was the jail. It was austere to the point of bareness. The desk, a chair, a rifle rack and a small wall cabinet were the sum total of the furnishing. Several cowboys were snoring in the cells. Hickok sat at the desk, smoking a long thin cigar.

'Find out anything, boy?' Hickok asked.

Angel nodded. 'I'd like to get my gun,' he said. Hickok got up and unlocked the cabinet, lifting Angel's Army Colt and belt out.

'I loaded it up for you,' he said. Angel looked his question.

'Had to let that cowboy go on bail, son,' the Marshal said. 'He never did nothing. His friend you beat up on went too. I guess they're around town somewhere. Wouldn't be surprised they were looking for you. So take my advice – get on your horse and sift some dust. I don't want to make a career out of pulling your chestnuts out o' the fire.'

'I never got the chance to thank you—' Angel began.

'No thanks needed, son. Despite what they say about me, I'd as soon avoid shootin' a man if it's possible.'

'I'm obliged,' Angel said.

'Wish you luck,' Hickok said. He did not offer his

hand, so Angel turned and went to the door. He went out into the darkening street and closed it behind him and as he did a voice across the street shouted 'OK, pilgrim!' and he saw the yellow lance of flame from the muzzle of a sixgun. Something touched his shoulder and then he was sitting on the sidewalk, his back hurting where he had smashed against the roughened bark of the jail-house wall. He fumbled for the gun at his hip as he heard footsteps running towards him.

'Kill the little bastard!' someone shouted.

SIX

Angel acted by blind instinct.

He rolled to the side, over and over and off the edge of the sidewalk into the dust, crying out as his wounded shoulder hit the hard earth. The gun was in his hand and he saw the two dark shapes running at him. Another shot boomed out and a huge chunk of splintered wood torn from the sidewalk went whirring past his face, tracing a long red finger across his cheekbone. He eared back the hammer of the Army Colt and the gun leaped in his hand, the roar blotting out sound. He saw one of the men slew to one side and go down kicking in the street as the other fired again and missed. He was on one knee now and he held the Colt steady in both hands, arms outstretched to their full limit and let the running figure come clear in the sights and then he released the hammer. The gun blasted again and it was almost as if he could see the line the bullet traced through the air. He saw the puff of dust clearly as the bullet struck the running man high on the chest and he went back as if he had been swatted. The gun flew from the man's hand, and Angel was up on his feet with the gun cocked again when Hickok came out around the back of the jailhouse, both guns in his hands.

'Stand still!' Hickok roared, and Angel froze. He let the barrel of the gun down.

'Uncock that thing and drop it!' Hickok yelled. 'Now!'

Angel complied, and Hickok came forward. He looked at Angel's shoulder and then at the two men in the street. One of them lay quite still. The other was writhing and groaning. Men were coming up the street warily, and Hickok watched them with eyes like a cat's, no movement escaping him.

'Bill!' someone yelled. 'It's Mike Williams. I'm coming through.'

'Get up here, man!' shouted the Marshal. A man pushed through the crowd with a shotgun canted ready in front of him. He turned and bayed the crowd as Hickok went out into the street and knelt down by the groaning man.

'Somebody get a doctor for this man!' he said as he straightened up. 'The rest of you get off the street. Move!' He gestured with the Navy Colts and the crowd melted back. 'Move, I said!' Hickok repeated, stalking towards them. The knot of people broke, retreating away from the tall marshal, and within a few minutes the sidewalk was empty again. Hickok turned to face Angel.

'Get into that office an' let me take a look at your arm,' he said brusquely. When Angel made a slight movement of demurral, Hickok cocked one of the Navy Colts loudly. 'Do like I say, son,' Hickok said softly. Angel nodded and went in as Hickok stooped to pick up all the fallen guns. He came in and turned up the lamp on the desk, slicing Angel's shirt away from the bloody shoulder with a wood-handled knife that had a blade about a foot long.

'Arkansas toothpick,' Hickok grinned, peering at Angel's shoulder.

'You're a fool for luck,' he pronounced. 'Just burned skin. Here . . . this ought to help.' He uncorked a whiskey bottle, sloshed some on his cupped hand, and slapped it on the gash in Angel's arm. Angel yelped, and Hickok grinned.

'Thank your lucky stars that's all the hurt you got,' he said. 'One day someone'll put a slug in you that's got to be taken out with a knife. Then you can really yell.'

He sat down at the desk and arrayed the three guns he had picked up in line abreast on it. He looked at them for a moment and then he looked up at Angel.

'You know what you've done,' he said.

'I had no choice,' Angel said. His arm was stinging like hell. 'You going to arrest me?'

'My job here is keeping the peace,' Hickok said. 'Right now, that means getting you out of town as fast as I can. Those were Texicans you burned down, sonny. This town is full of their friends. You want to stay and discuss the question of self-defence with two hundred of them when they've had time to likker up an' come lookin' for you?'

'Not much,' Angel admitted. 'Not very much at all.'

'What I thought,' Hickok said. 'That's the first good sense I've heard out o' you since I set eyes on you.'

'Will it make trouble for you?' Angel wanted to know. Hickok's eyes crinkled at the corners. 'I've known it happen,' he said. 'Them cowboys aren't what you could call my staunchest admirers.'

'Then—'

'—then nothing!' Hickok said. 'There won't be any trouble I can't handle. As long as you're not around. Tell me – where did you learn to shoot like that?'

Angel shook his head. 'I didn't even know what I was doing,' he said.

Hickok nodded. 'Fools for luck,' he sighed. 'Well, boy, you got to git. And fast. Only one thing more I can do for you.' He gestured at the guns on his desk and Angel reached for the Army Colt.

He was still reaching for the gun when he heard the

door open and he whirled like a cat, the Army Colt coming up cocked and ready. The man in the doorway was Hickok's deputy, Mike Williams. He stood mouth agape, the shotgun dangling in his right hand, as Hickok burst out laughing. Angel put the gun up, shrugging shamefacedly as Williams came into the office.

'Meet Mike Williams,' Hickok grinned. 'Special policeman at the Novelty. He helps me out, sometimes. Mike – you nearly got separated from yourself then. Maybe you'll remember what I'm always tellin' you – never come up unexpected behind a man with a gun in his hand!'

Williams shook his head. 'I'll remember next time,' he said, smiling. 'Son, you sure are nervous. Put that thing away, will you?'

Angel pushed the gun into its holster and then strapped the rig on around his waist. Hickok gestured at the other guns on the desk. There was a beaten-up Navy 1851 and a pocket Colt, the 1848 model with engraved sideplates.

'You could take those,' he offered. 'Those fellows won't be needin' them any more.'

'I'll stick to this,' Angel said.

Hickok smiled. 'You may be right at that, way you handled it. Mike, you look after things here a while, will you?' He asked Angel where he had left his horse and Angel told him. 'I'll walk this youngster down to A Street. He's leavin' town and I do mean now.'

Williams nodded. 'Good thinking,' he told Angel.

They walked outside. Texas Street was bright with flaring oil lamps and the saloons were roaring. Honkytonk pianos were barrelling away, and coarse shouts of laughter and pleasure came from the bright doorways. The sidewalks were crowded but Angel noticed that a respectful path was always made for Hickok. They walked as far as the railway depot and then the Marshal stopped.

'Far as I go – alone,' he said. 'You got any money, son?'

Angel nodded. 'All I need,' he lied.

'Here's a stake, anyway,' Hickok said, pressing a coin into his hand.

'Don't argue, just take it. It won't hurt to have an Angel thinkin' good of me.' The younger man could see his wry grin in the flaring lights of Texas Street. Hickok did not extend his hand.

'Where you headin', Angel?'

'New Mexico,' Angel said.

'Good,' was the reply. 'Don't ever come into one of my towns again. *Sabe?*'

'You got a deal,' Angel said. 'Good luck, Mr Hickok.'

'I can use all there is,' Hickok said and turned back towards Texas Street.

SEVEN

He cut their trail in Raton.

There had been a fracas in the saloon, and several people remembered the squint-eyed man called Milt who had tried to pistolwhip a man he thought was cutting in on his conversation with one of the girls. A heavyset, black-haired man had intervened, and when the sheriff had turned up, smoothed things over by saying they were moving out right away heading for Las Vegas.

It figured, Angel thought.

Cravetts and his men had been out for a long time, and there was money from the Fort Riley robbery burning a hole in their jeans. They would head somewhere they could spend it. Las Vegas might hold them for a while. Two days later he rode into the town and hitched his horse outside the Plaza Hotel. There were shade trees planted in the square, and everywhere the indolent air of Spain: it was like another world after the flat harshness of Kansas and the cool heights of Colorado. Somewhere in one of the low-lying adobes across the square he could hear a woman laughing, and the random strum of a guitar came from one of the *cantinas*.

He asked for a room, and the desk clerk pushed the book across for him to sign. Frank Angel scanned it

49

quickly, but the scribbled names gave him no clues. He needed time.

The clerk sent a Mexican out to take care of the horse and Angel paid him in advance for the room. He went out again into the square and methodically visited the *cantinas* one by one. His eyes checked off every white man he saw – for there were many shades of skin here: Indian, Mexican, even one or two Negro troopers from Fort Union – but saw no one who gave him any faint flutter of recognition. In the *cantinas* though, they all looked at him.

Frank Angel was tall, and wide-shouldered, and the cold eyes had the look of a wary wolf in them. His travel-stained clothes, hard used on the long journey, and the old Army Colt slung high on the right hip drew attention. Men like him were hardly rare in places like this: but the look on his face, the way his right hand stayed always near the revolver, set him apart.

He had to start somewhere, so he went back to the hotel. The desk clerk looked up when he spun the gold coin Hickok had given him on the desk, and made change for it without comment.

'Where's the best place in town for poker?' Angel asked him. The clerk didn't sneer but he came close to it.

'The big games,' he said, emphasizing the adjective, 'are at the Cattleman, down the street, two doors along from the *Optic* offices.'

Angel looked his question.

'The *Optic*, the newspaper,' the clerk explained impatiently. 'But I was you, I'd try one of the *cantinas*. Twenty bucks won't get you more than two hands at the Cattleman.'

'Big stakes, huh?' Angel said.

'You could say that,' the clerk said. 'Take my tip an' try

something more your size, son.'

'I might at that,' Angel replied and went out into the plaza. He walked down to the southern end and turned left along the street. The stores and business buildings were dark now, closed tight for the night, but here and there pools of light spilled out on to the sidewalk from *cantinas*, and throngs of passers-by bustled from one saloon to the next. The Cattleman was a brick building with plate glass windows on both sides of the batwing doors, crowded inside with tables and chairs, a long bar going the length of the building on the left hand side. In back of the room, a round table with a green felt top was lit by an overhead lamp, and around it sat seven men. Kibitzers crowded around the table, which was littered with poker chips, glasses and bottles. Cigar smoke wreathed upwards towards the light, where dozens of moths fluttered around the hot glass.

Frank Angel bought a drink at the bar and carried it across the room to where he could lean against the back wall of the saloon and watch the game. The stakes, as the desk clerk had warned him, were big enough: he reckoned there was about forty dollars in the pot. The dealer was a thickset man with a black broadcloth coat and a fancy vest across which a gold watch chain was linked. His hands were cleft as they flicked cards to each of the players, two deeply-tanned men, obviously local ranchers, a slim young fellow with his hat tilted forward over his eyes, an elderly man with grizzled hair whom the dealer referred to as 'Doc', a middle-aged man in a blue serge business suit, and a narrow-shouldered man of about forty who sat with his back towards Frank Angel and drank regularly from the bottle on the table in front of him.

Angel stood and watched the game for an hour, nursing his drink. He listened as the conversation ebbed and flowed between hands, putting names to the players. The dealer's name was Singer, he learned. The two ranchers, although they did not look at all alike, were brothers, Brian and Peter something. A few rough jokes here and there established the fact that 'Doc' was the town's doctor, and the man with the hat tilted over his face was called Kamins. The narrow-shouldered man now drawing to a pair of sevens was the only one for whom Angel did not have a name, but as the dealer flicked the cards across the table the one called Kamins said 'Come on, Milt, see if you can get some o' your money back.'

'Hell, Kamins, he ain't lost that much,' Singer expostulated.

'If you call five hundred not much,' the one called Milt growled, 'you ought to let me know what much is, some time.'

'Aw, play cards or fold, Sharp,' one of the ranchers said. At the last word, Angel straightened up and then edged around until he could see Sharp's face. The man looked up at him and their eyes met. Milt Sharp had a peculiar cast to his eyes, Angel realized. It wasn't exactly a squint, but you had the curious impression that he was looking just past you when in fact he was looking at you.

'What the hell you starin' at?' he snapped at Angel.

'Sorry,' Angel said, holding up a hand in the peace sign. 'Just waiting for a chance to sit in.'

'You can sit in soon enough if I don't get some cards soon,' growled Sharp. 'I can't do a thing with this shit.'

'You bettin' or foldin', Sharp?' complained the dealer.

'He's doin' whatever he wants to do, Singer,' said the one called Kamins softly. There was no edge to his voice at all, but Singer looked at him sharply and paled visibly.

'See here, Howie,' he said, 'no call for that kind of talk.'

'Then let Milt play his hand the way he wants to,'

Kamins said amiably.

'Sure, Howie, sure,' Singer hastened to say. 'No hurry. No hurry at all.'

Kamins looked up across the table. He pushed back the Stetson with his thumb, exposing a bright thatch of auburn hair, growing thick and sharp to a widow's peak in the centre of his forehead.

'I reckon I'll quit after this hand, Milt,' he said. 'Just not my night.'

'Mine, neither!' scowled Sharp, slamming his cards down on the table and taking a gulp of the whiskey from his bottle. If they noticed Angel leave the saloon by the rear entrance they did not react. They waited for the hand to finish and then got up, saying their grumbling farewells to the other players with the joking words that expressed good fellowship but in fact concealed their seething rage at losing to what Sharp kept constantly referring to as 'small town hicks'. They came out into the street arguing, Sharp's voice slurred and angry, Kamins talking soothingly, reasonably.

They walked along the street until they came to the plaza. Sharp was still sulking over his losses at the card table.

'Bastards,' he said and spat on the sidewalk.

'Sure, Milt,' Kamins said. 'But no trouble, right? That's what we said. A nice layover. A few drinks, some girls – an' no trouble. We told Dick: no trouble.'

'I know,' Sharp said after a moment. 'It ain't the money, it's . . .'

'Come on Milt,' Kamins grinned in the darkness. 'It ain't as if it was your own money.' The two men laughed.

'Hey,' Sharp said. 'I got an idea. Let's go over to Angela's.'

'Jesus, Milt, you must have had every *puta* in town twice,' Kamins said. 'You still lookin' for more?'

'Keeps you healthy,' Sharp leered. 'You comin' or not?'

'I'm going back to the hotel,' Kamins told him. 'You go get laid if you've a mind to. I need a drink.'

They stepped off the sidewalk into the wide dusty street and as they did so Angel stepped off the walk on the opposite corner and came towards them. When they were about twenty feet apart he stopped.

'You two!' he said. 'Hold it right there!'

Kamins stopped dead but Sharp leaned forward blearily and said petulantly 'What the hell is this?'

'I'm going to kill one of you,' Angel said flatly.

'Ain't that the kid that was watchin' the card game?' Kamins said, his voice cool and unpanicked. Then to Angel: 'What beef you got with us, boy?' He started to walk towards Angel, his hands spread in an attitude of reasonable inquiry but Angel stopped him with his next words.

'I'm from Kansas,' he told them.

Sharp swore and moved as he did so, his hand stabbing for the gun in the holster at his side. In the same moment Kamins grabbed for the gun in his shoulder holster. He was about two seconds behind Sharp and in that time Angel shot Sharp very coolly through the top of the head and Kamins screamed as he was splattered with the grey-black ooze from Sharp's shattered skull. The gun he had yanked out of his shoulder holster went off wild, and then he cocked it again, but now Angel had run across the space between them, lightfooted as an Apache, swinging the long-barrelled Colt in a looping arc that ended in a vicious, smashing blow just above Kamins' ear. The red-haired man went down to the ground in a thrashing heap of arms and legs, dust boiling up in a cloud as he rolled helplessly, half-conscious. Angel kicked away the gun which had fallen to the ground and stood above the fallen man. There were shouts along the street, and men were coming out of the saloons. He heard feet running along the wooden sidewalks, hoarse shouts.

'Where's Cravetts?' Angel snapped at the fallen Kamins, who was trying to sit up, shaking his head. Angel kneeled down and jammed the barrel of his gun under Kamins' chin, jerking the man's head back.

'Where are they?' he repeated. 'Where's Cravetts and the rest of them?'

'Who . . . who are you?' Kamins managed.

'You've got ten seconds to answer my question, Kamins. Or I'm going to kill you.' Angel said it without any attempt at bluster. It came out icy and convincing.

'Santa Fé!' he gasped. 'They were heading for Santa Fé!'

'Where after that?'

'I dunno,' Kamins muttered. There was a lot of activity in the street now. He knew help was on the way, and his courage was returning. There was no chance of his being shot in front of twenty or thirty bystanders. 'Kamins,' Angel said warningly. 'You better tell me.'

'Go to hell, kid,' Kamins said, and Angel shot him through the knee. The man screamed in blinded agony as the bullet smashed the bones of his leg, and as Angel had expected, the sound of the shot drove the oncoming townsfolk back towards shelter. They receded into the shadows along the street, into doorways and saloon porches, awaiting developments. A man didn't prove anything by getting himself shot, knocked down by a stray bullet. Vegas had a sheriff. Let him handle it.

Kamins was moaning in agony in the dust on Santa Fé Street. Angel looked dispassionately at him.

'Now: the truth,' he said.

Kamins loosed off a stream of obscenities, every foul

55

thing he could lay his tongue to being directed at the flint-faced man standing over him.

'You got ten seconds, Howie,' Angel said. 'Then you get it in the other leg.'

'You wouldn't do that!' Kamins gasped. 'You wouldn't deliberately make a man a cripple for life.'

'Try me,' Frank Angel said and cocked the Army Colt.

'Who . . . who are you?' Kamins managed. His face was still screwed tight with the pain from his leg, both hands gripping the hurt limb fiercely.

'You never heard of me,' the younger man said. 'My name is Frank Angel and you've got five seconds.'

'Angel?' Kamins was playing for time and Angel knew it.

'Three,' he said.

Kamins looked into the empty eyes and watched as Angel raised the gun.

'No,' he choked. 'I'll tell you!'

'Make it good, Howie,' Angel said softly. He knelt down and laid the barrel of the gun against Kamins' good leg. 'And make it fast.'

'Santa Fé,' Kamins gasped, hastily. 'They was goin' to lay over a while in Santa Fé, get fresh horses. Torelli has a brother in Socorro.'

'Torelli? Who's Torelli?'

'Frank Torelli,' Kamins said, 'one of the boys.'

'Give me all their names,' Angel said. 'Every man on the Fort Riley job.'

'There was me, Milt—' Kamins turned to look at Sharp's shattered head and shuddered. 'Cravetts, Monsher, Vister and Juba.'

'First names,' snapped Angel. 'Come on, come on!'

'Dick Cravetts, Lee Monsher, Johnnie Vister, Denny Juba!' Kamins rushed. 'Listen, you got to get me to doctor!'

'Sure,' Angel said. 'Where does Cravetts hail from?'

'Arizona,' Kamins said. 'Tucson way, I think.'

'How much did you boys lift from the Army payroll?'

'About sixteen thousand,' Kamins muttered. 'Listen, Angel, I ain't talkin' no more till you get me a doctor. I'm gonna bleed to death.'

'No chance,' Angel said, and, shot him through the heart. Kamins went back down flat and hard, and Angel heard someone shout in alarm. The people who had been watching from the safety of the ramadas on the sidewalk about thirty or forty feet away scampered back out of range to the safety of their doorways. Along the street Angel heard the sound of running feet. Someone in the darkness shouted 'It's the sheriff!'

He had only moments. Without hesitation or shame he rifled Kamins' coat pockets, and then Sharp's. Both men had wallets stuffed with banknotes and both had pokes of what felt like gold dust. He jammed everything into his pockets and ran for the tree-filled plaza, where the shadows were like the bottomless pits of Hell.

'Hey, you!' he heard someone shout.

He had traced his return path carefully earlier in the evening and knew every step of the way even in the pitch blackness of the empty square. He came out of the trees on the northern side of the plaza and crossed over to the ramada of the hotel. A group of men was standing in the doorway craning their necks to see what the fuss was down the street. He came up behind them and asked a question. A burly man in a business suit looked him up and down.

'Some kind of fracas down the street,' he said. At that moment the desk clerk came up the sidewalk from the direction of the street and the men outside the hotel clustered around him, Angel among them.

'Two men shot dead down there,' the clerk was saying

excitedly. 'Some feller shot them dead and robbed them right in the middle of the street!'

'Anyone see who it was?' someone asked.

'I dunno,' the clerk said. 'Sheriff's down there now!'

'I reckon I'll go down there take a look,' another man said. 'You comin', Harry?'

'Hell with it,' the man called Harry said. 'It ain't no concern o' mine. Someone gets his liver shot out once a week in this burg.'

The knot of people began to dissolve. Some went down the walk towards the scene of the affray, others went back inside the hotel. Angel went in with them and asked the clerk for his key. The clerk handed it to him without even taking time to look at Angel. He was anxious to get back to talking about what had happened.

Angel went to his room and locked the door. He sat on the bed and waited a long time until his hands stopped shaking. Much, much later he fell asleep fully dressed.

EIGHT

The office of the Attorney-General of the United States was a spacious, high-ceilinged room. It was on the first floor of the huge building on Pennsylvania Avenue in Washington which housed the Department of Justice. The office was in many ways a reflection of the character of the man who occupied it. One wall was covered with shelves in which books of all kinds were stacked, upright and flat, face forward and spine out, books on criminal law and international law, books on psychology, criminology, natural history, sociology and many more, books which showed the signs of much use and a complete disregard on the part of their owner to treat them as anything but what they were: tools, part of his job. A huge desk dominated the right hand corner of the room, and two floor-to-ceiling windows looked out on the bustle of traffic in the muddy mess of Pennsylvania Avenue. Two armchairs with dark leather upholstery were ranged in front of the desk. The only other furniture was a huge oak cupboard and an iron safe with an ornate scrollwork of brass. On the wall behind the desk was the circular seal of the Department of Justice.

The Attorney-General tossed aside the sheaf of buff coloured reports he had been reading and slapped the desk in anger. The man in the armchair opposite blinked but let no expression cross his face.

'Two months!' the Attorney-General said angrily. 'Two months – and not a trace! Not a smell! Nothing! What the devil are we doing?'

'Everything we can, chief,' the man in the armchair said quietly. He was a big man, wide across the shoulders and still for all his forty-five years, narrow-waisted and lithe, his frame indicating that he would probably move with catlike grace and speed if he had to. He had a tanned face, lines scoured into it by years in the open, and the clear blue eyes of a boy. His hair was a dark blond and he wore the customary fashionable moustache. Dressed in ordinary city clothes, he looked, apart from the outdoor tan, like any other city dweller. In fact he was the Chief Investigator of the United States Department of Justice. His name was Angus Wells.

'Well, it isn't good enough, Angus,' the Attorney-General said.

'Haven't the Provost-Marshal's office come up with anything?'

'Just the names,' Wells replied. 'They're in the report.'

'Anything known?'

'Like it says,' Wells told him. 'Cravetts was in the California Column. Mustered out in Fort Stanton, New Mexico in '66. That's all we have.'

'Not enough,' grunted the Attorney-General. He reached over his desk and took a long, black cigar from the box on his right, then offered it, as an afterthought, to Wells. The latter shook his head as the Attorney-General set fire to the cigar. He had once unwisely accepted one of those cigars; they tasted like a mixture of tarred rope and horse blankets. The Attorney-General inhaled with every indication of huge enjoyment and blew a cloud of smoke towards the ceiling.

'Not enough at all. You've read all this stuff, of

course?' He gestured with his cigar towards the sheaf of papers on his desk.

'Nothing much there either,' Wells said. 'The Provost-Marshal's people did the best they could, but there was really nothing to follow up. They robbed the paymaster's wagon at Fort Riley, then turned up at a ranch near Fort Dodge, where they killed two men and raped a woman, stealing ten horses. After that they disappeared. Nobody saw them. All we have are sketchy descriptions provided by the woman—'

'Mrs Gibbons?'

'—that's right, sir, and the names of the men.'

'What about this youngster who pulled her out of the house. The hired hand, what was his name?' He shuffled through the papers and picked out something with his finger. 'Angel. Frank Angel. Could he have been involved in any way?'

'Inside man, you mean?' Wells shook his head. 'I doubt it. The Army people at Fort Larned spoke very highly of him.'

'And. . . ?'

'And nothing. He seems to have dropped out of sight.'

The Attorney-General tapped his teeth with the smouldering cigar.

'Interesting,' he said.

'Not really, sir,' Wells replied. 'By all accounts he was just a young fellow without any family. He probably drifted off looking for another job somewhere. Could be anywhere in Kansas.'

The Attorney-General shrugged. 'If you think so,' he said. 'But I want some action on this, Angus. If that gang gets off scot-free, they'll hit another payroll somewhere, or a bank, or a mining shipment. Look at all the trouble down there in Missouri with this guerilla gang.'

'In Clay County, you mean? The James-Younger

bunch? That's just local stuff,' Wells said.

The Attorney-General shook his head. 'No, Angus, you're wrong. They'll cross a State line, sooner or later. Iowa, perhaps, or Kansas. Then they'll be our problem.'

'You may be right,' Wells said.

'Damn sure of it,' the Attorney-General said. 'That's why I want this Cravetts bunch brought in. Nipped in the bud, stopped now. Before they get the taste for it.'

Wells nodded. 'You want me to get on to it myself.' It wasn't a question and the Attorney-General nodded.

'As soon as you can,' he said. 'When can you start?'

'I can be in Fort Riley by the middle of the week,' Wells replied.

The Attorney-General looked up, surprise in his eyes. Then he smiled.

'No, no, Angus,' he said. 'We're going to play this one a little more cunningly. You'll never backtrack that bunch. The trail is two months old. I want you to try something else.'

Wells leaned forward. He liked to see the Chief's mind working: his hunches were legendary.

'Fort Stanton, New Mexico,' the Attorney-General said, almost dreamily. 'Start there. And work forwards. My hunch is you'll meet them coming in instead of chasing them halfway across the country.'

'It's worth a try,' Wells said. 'I'll get started.'

'You'll have to do better than just try, Angus,' the man in the chair by the big window said flatly. 'I want this wrapped up and I want it wrapped up very soon, and I want it wrapped up by this Department and not the Army. Do I make myself clear?'

Wells nodded, and went out of the office. The Attorney-General's secretary was sitting in the anteroom, copying some reports. She looked up and smiled.

Wells shook his head. 'Phew!' he said.

Miss Rowe smiled again. She'd never seen one of the Department's Investigators come out of that room yet with a smile on his face.

NINE

He rode in past San Miguel Church.

Children playing in the dusty streets outside huddled *jacals* called to him as he rode by, and the men lounging in the shade of the plaza's big cottonwoods eyed him beneath tilted sombreros as he hitched his horse outside the hotel.

Frank Angel had come a long way, and he looked different now to the youngster who had set out so many weeks ago from Fort Larned. There was a different air about him. A lot of the boyishness was gone from the face, to be replaced by a wolflike angling of the jaws and a cold, wary look in the pale eyes that said, as clearly as if the word was written on his forehead: hunter.

The trail he was on was much warmer now. There were fewer places for his quarry to be, and where they had passed, people had recalled *los gringos*. At Herlow's Hotel on San Francisco Street in old Santa Fé, they had purchased new horses. Old Herlow had been happy to describe them, and their riders, to the cold-eyed inquisitor, happier still to accept the twenty dollars Angel gave him for his help. He had brought a new horse himself – a rangy, lineback dun with plenty of stamina. He had new clothes, bought as had been the horse with the money he had taken without shame from the men he had killed in

64

Las Vegas. He did not think much about the rights and wrongs of the way he had killed them. They were a species of vermin. Only a fool would release a trapped rat to breed another generation of rats.

Socorro was quieter these days than it had been when the mining boom had been on, but it was still a bustling, lively town. Big rambling adobes fronted on to the plaza, and the streets were busy with pack trains heading up into the Magdalenas or moving carefully south towards the Jornado del Muerto.

He went into the *cantina* next to the hotel.

'A beer,' he said. 'The coldest one in the place.'

'*Sí, señor*,' grinned the bartender. He drew the beer and put it on the rough bar, the foam slopping over the sides of the glass. After the hard dry heat of the desert, it was like drinking iced nectar. Angel drank it down in one long swallow and put the glass down, motioning the barkeep to fill it up again. He looked around. There were only a few people in the place, most of them Mexicans.

'Have one yourself,' Angel said to the man behind the bar, and watched while the man filled a glass. 'Where's the bank here?'

The bartender directed him across the plaza and he walked through the tree-shaded square across to the solid adobe building which housed the First National Bank of Santa Fé. He pushed inside into the welcome cool gloom.

There was a counter with a grille in front of it, a door to one side. He asked to see the manager.

The man came out of the office. He was a slender man of about forty, a neatly-trimmed beard and florid face.

'How can I help you, sir?' he said.

'I'd like to get some coin for this,' Angel said, handing the man the buckskin bag of gold dust he had taken off

Kamins. The manager hefted it in his hand. His eyes flickered over Angel briefly as he set up the scales.

'Stranger in these parts?' he asked.

'Passing through,' Angel replied. 'Heading for Mesilla.'

'So,' the bank manager said. 'I make this a shade over four hundred and thirty dollars. You want coin or paper?'

'Paper will do,' Angel said. The man nodded, and went through into the open area behind the counter, opening a drawer and counting out some notes. He locked the drawer and came back into his office.

'You may be able to help me,' Angel said. 'I'm looking for a place owned by a man named Torelli. You know it?'

The manager looked at him differently. There was surprise in his eyes and a curl of distaste on his full lips.

'You know the Torellis?' he asked.

'Never met them,' Angel said. 'Friend in Santa Fé told me I should look them up.'

'Listen, Mister – ah?' Angel supplied his name. 'Mr Angel, if I may speak frankly, I'd recommend you leave your money with us here at the bank if you're going to the Torelli place.

Angel looked his question.

'It's a road ranch, Mr Angel. One of those – ah, places, you know, they have, ah – girls there, cheap liquor. It – they have a very unsavoury reputation, sir. I could not let you go there without at least warning you. It isn't the kind of place a gentleman would go to. No, not at all. A thoroughly bad lot, the Torellis.'

'Tell me about them,' Angel suggested. The manager warmed to the task. He obviously felt strongly about the bad influence people like the Torellis had on the character of the town. He told Angel that there had originally been three brothers, all of Italian origin, who had come west from New York at the time of the mining boom. They had enough money to buy a rundown old spread about six miles south of town, and it had become a Mecca for the miners down from the Magdalenas with dust in their pockets to spend, for teamsters and outlaws coming in off the Jornado, dry as a bone and looking for fun.

'They haven't quite the character to be badmen,' the manager told him. 'One of them, Bill Torelli, was hanged right here in town a few years ago. He tried to bust up a poker game he was in and shot a man in the hand. The miners strung him up from one of the beams in the hotel and put a notice on him: "Hanged for being a damned nuisance!" The other two brothers made noises about coming up here and taking revenge on the town, but a bunch of men from the town rode down there and sorted them out. Franco ran for it. He didn't even have the nerve to stay and face the posse. The third brother, Steve – his real name is Stefano – came to a sort of agreement with the townspeople. He would keep his girls and his friends out of Socorro and Socorro would leave him alone. There were some of us, I should tell you, who thought that was a mistake. We ought to have burned the place down. At any rate, it's still there, and a filthy dirty dump it is. My advice, Mr Angel, would be to steer clear of it.'

Angel had listened carefully to the man's gossip. If Socorro was like other towns in the west, the road ranch would be tolerated because it kept the hookers out of town itself, where they could offend the local people. Better that than the way it was on Texas Street in Abilene, where the whores jostled the decent women and spat at them.

'This Franco,' he asked. 'He never came back?'

'Not that I've ever heard,' the bank manager said. 'I

did hear once he was working in the railway yards at Kansas City, but I don't know whether it was true or not. I never imagined any of them doing an honest day's work.'

Angel picked up his hat and rose.

'I'm obliged for your help,' he told the manager. 'Maybe I'll steer clear of the Torelli place after all. One last question: you know a man called Cravetts, Dick Cravetts?' He described the man. The bank manager pursed his lips, thought awhile, then shook his head ruefully.

'Afraid not,' he said. 'I know most people in Socorro, but the name's not one I've heard before.'

'No matter,' Angel said. 'I'll find him.'

He went out of the bank, and the bank manager found for some reason that he suddenly felt chilled. He went out into the plaza and stood for a moment in the sunshine, watching as Frank Angel swung aboard the lineback and moved on to the street, heading south. There was something about the man which he could not quite define, and it bothered him. It was much later that he associated the feeling with the chill he had felt when Angel had said, very quietly, that he would find the man he was looking for.

The road ranch was built in a clump of cottonwoods between the road and the river. It was an unlovely place, and nobody had wasted any money on paint for it. The boards were whitened and bleached by years of merciless sun, the sprawling frame building askew here and there with warped uprights. A hitching rack ran the length of the front and two steps led up on to a shaded ramada. There was a corral off to the right at the back of the place. There were half a dozen horses switching their tails idly against the persistent flies, heads low. He tied up at the hitching rail and pushed in through the door.

The place was almost empty. At a table in the corner a drunk lay head on table, a glass overturned in front of his folded arms. Two teamsters were arguing friendlily over a beer at the bar. There were two girls in short skirts at another table and they looked up as Angel came in, pasting smiles on their wan faces. He heard them whispering together, and eventually one of them got up and came over to him. She was petite, dark-haired, sloe-eyed. Mixed blood, Angel figured, some Indian, some Mexican, maybe even some Anglo, it was hard to tell. Her skin was that smooth brown that does not give away age. He figured she was about twenty-two, which was in fact four years older than she actually was.

'Hello mister,' the girl said. 'Buy a girl a drink?'

He smiled down at her. 'Sure,' he said. 'What's your name?'

'Carmen,' she said.

'Frank,' he replied. He fished out a twenty-dollar piece and spun it on the bar. The bartender, a fishy-eyed man of about fifty, served the two whiskies Angel ordered. It was cheap rotgut and he guessed that what the girl had was cold tea. She touched his thigh boldly.

'You goin' to stay awhile?' she asked.

'I might,' Angel told her. 'Is Torelli here?'

'Which one?' she said, then her hand flew to her mouth. She looked at the bartender but he appeared not to have heard what she said. Her eyes were wide and she looked at Angel, whose face showed nothing.

'I know he's here, Carmen,' he said, softly. 'No need for you to get involved. It's Frank I want. Where is he?'

'Upstairs,' she whispered. 'Oh, God, mister, there goin' to be trouble?'

'Depends entirely on him,' Angel told her. 'You want

69

to go and tell him there's a man down here called Frank Angel who's come to kill him?'

The bartender caught that and he started to duck below the level of the bar, but before he had even gotten halfway, he froze. The big bore of the Army Colt stared right back at him. The girl gasped. She had not seen the movement of Angel's hand.

'Lissen, mister,' the bartender said, putting his hands squarely on the rough pine bar. 'Any shootin' in here, innocent people is gonna get hurt. You got a beef with someone, you take it outside.'

Angel shook his head. 'Wrong,' he told the man. 'Take yourself outside, and take the girls with you. It's Frank Torelli I want. No need for anyone else to get hurt.'

He turned to the girl. 'Go on up and tell him what I told you. Then stay up there. Don't come back down here. *Comprende?*'

She nodded and started up the stairs. The barkeep came warily around his bar and edged towards the door. Angel let him go, taking the other girl with him. The two teamsters who had been drinking beer rousted the drunk out of his slumbers and half-dragged, half-carried him outside. Angel could see them straining to see through the grimy windows. He waited at the bar, his eyes fixed on the stairs. He felt empty. Someone he had never seen in his life was going to come to the top of that staircase and he was going to kill him – or get killed trying. He supposed he ought to feel some kind of guilt, or inbred reluctance to consider taking the life of another man. He felt only the steady throb of his own determination. This Torelli had been one of the men at the Gibbons place. What had been done there was enough to merit death. He loosened the Army Colt in its holster and eased away from the bar. A fly was buzzing

70

against the window. He could hear the tick of a clock somewhere. Then the man appeared at the top of the stairs.

TEN

Angus Wells got lucky in Lincoln.

He spent three days talking to the commanding officer at Fort Stanton, his brother officers, enlisted men, to the post traders Murphy and Dolan. Murphy, a Satanic-looking, hard-drinking Irishman, had held officer rank in the Army and was known universally as 'the Colonel'. He had served in Carleton's California Column and remembered Richard Cravetts. He told Wells that the ex-Captain had settled on a ranch in the Tularosa Valley in the late sixties, and been raided out by Mescaleroes.

'Lost track of him after that,' he recalled, pouring another liberal glassful of whiskey out and drinking it greedily. They were sitting in the rambling building on the edge of the sprawled fort, looking out at the parade ground, dazzling white in the burning sun.

'You sure you won't have another, Mr Wells?' Murphy asked.

Wells shook his head and Murphy poured himself another drink. It seemed to make no difference to his speech or posture.

'We've been having our own troubles in these parts,' Murphy went on. 'Lot of rustling, some killings over at Placita – Lincoln, they call it now – the county seat. Old John Chisum's jingle-bob warriors take it hard when someone steals their boss's beef.' He grinned as if it was a huge joke. 'But I recall Cravetts had some real trouble over in Lincoln. A shooting affair, as I recall. You ought to ride over and talk to Ham Mills, the sheriff. He'll probably be able to tell you more.'

Wells rode across the hills to the little town of Lincoln. It lay athwart a noisy stream called the Bonito, straggling along a street shaped like a flattened S, adobes and crude shacks well spaced on both sides. Ham Mills was a huge man, with a white scar on his jaw. He scratched his head awhile, then plunged into the welter of papers and books in his old roll-topped desk. Eventually he found the document he was looking for.

'Here you go,' he said. 'Cravetts, Richard. Assault with a deadly weapon, intent to kill. I remember that now.' He leaned back in his chair. 'Early last year, it was. He came up here to sell some horses. Him and another fellow, young tough with tow hair an' a Southern accent. Lee something.'

'Monsher?' Wells supplied, and Mills smacked his thigh with a hand like a hammer. 'Monsher it was!' he said. 'Bad lot, I reckoned.'

'What happened?' Wells asked.

'Forget the details,' Mills said. 'But I recall it was in Patron's place. Some *hombre* named Goss, Gross, somethin' like that, came to me an' claimed Cravetts an' that Monsher feller stole his horses off his ranch down Alamogordo way, wanted me to get his money off of them. I told him he'd have to swear out a complaint afore the justice, "Green" Wilson, but he swore at me an' said he didn't have no time for that kind o' fiddlefaddle. Next I know he went down Patron's saloon an' called those two jaspers out. There was a shootin' and Cravetts an' Monsher lit out, leavin' Goss three parts dead.'

'Didn't anyone try to stop them?'

'Oh, sure,' Mills said. 'We got out a posse an' chased them clear across to Three Rivers, but they headed out into the malpais, an' you couldn't track a elephant in the White Sands, mister.'

Wells nodded. He knew the vast and featureless expanse that was called White Sands. Hundreds and hundreds of square miles of glaring white gypsum sand stretched from Socorro in the north almost as far south as the San Agustin Pass through the Organ Mountains. Men who did not want to be caught could find no better refuge from pursuers than that trackless waste.

'Have you any idea where Cravetts and Monsher came from?' Wells asked. 'They told me over at the Fort that Cravetts used to have a ranch in the Tularosa valley.'

'Afore my time,' Mills told him. 'I heerd they was from out Arizona Territory. Lordsburg was what I heerd.'

'Lordsburg,' Wells said. 'Sounds likely, anyway.'

'Likelier than they'd stay in Lincoln County anyways,' Mills told him.

'I still got a warrant out on both them jaspers they ever show their faces around here again.' Wells rose to leave. 'I'm obliged to you, Sheriff.'

'No trouble,' Mills said. 'You ketch up with them jaspers, let me know. We got a quiet little town here an' I aim to keep it that way.'

Wells headed on out of the sleepy little placita and up the canyon towards Fort Stanton. It was a long way to Mesilla and well over a hundred miles to Lordsburg from there. He kicked his horse into a run.

ELEVEN

The man on the stairs had his hands above his head.

'You, mister!' he shouted. 'I ain't armed. Don't shoot!' He was short and pudgy, and the light from the grimy windows flickered on his eyeglasses. Angel could see the man's tongue nervously touching thick, rubbery lips.

'Where's Torelli?' he said flatly.

'He – I – he's not here, mister,' the man said. He started down the stairs, eyes fixed on Angel, moving carefully, slowly. He kept talking all the way down as though by talking he could prevent anything from happening to him.

'Torelli ain't here, mister,' the man droned. 'He left earlier this mornin'. Headed for Las Cruces. That stupid Carmen thought she seen him upstairs but it was me she seen, not Frank.' He kept on coming down the stairs and Angel watched him every inch of the way. He watched the man's eyes and when he saw them flicker towards the window he moved, one swift leap lifting him over the top of the bar and behind it as the glass from one of the windows shattered inwards with the booming roar of a gun and Angel heard the fat smack of the slivered slug hitting the other side of the bar. He went sideways along the floor, stretching upwards to where he had earlier seen the bartender reaching, his hand closing on the stock of a shotgun. He pulled it down, still rolling, as the man on the staircase ran into the space in front of the bar, a sixgun in his hand, pumping shots, scrabbling in the blaze of noise to get around behind the bar and at Angel. Angel eared back the hammers on the shotgun, whose barrels were sawn off at about the ten inch mark, and as the man came around the bar, eyes glaring behind the spectacles, lining the gun down on the squirming Angel, he pulled both triggers. The awful flat *voommmph!* sounded like a thunderclap in the enclosed space and the close-packed shot had spread only about a foot when it hit the thick-lipped one. It tore a hole in his upper body the size of a plate and hurled him back against the wall with a force that shook the building. In the same instant, guns blasted from the doorway as two men came running crouched into the room, diving for the shelter of tipped-over tables, laying down a hail of bullets where they thought Angel was. But Angel had moved and he came up above the counter and threw two shots fast at the man on the left, who lurched in mid-stride as he went down behind cover, his legs kicking high and a bubbling scream of pain breaking from his lips. The third man fired hastily at Angel, scrabbling back away from the side of the room towards the door. Angel went down again on the boards behind the bar, squirming on his elbows towards the huddled body of the man with the eyeglasses. There was a huge, sticky puddle of blood staining the splintered duckboards but Angel ignored it as he wormed towards the open end of the bar. Before he reached it he heard the frantic scramble of boots and leaped to his feet in time to throw an unaimed shot after the man who burst out of the door. Angel's bullet took a huge chunk of wood out of the door frame and then his target was outside. He heard running feet and shouts from the bartender and the girls outside. He ran catlike towards the door and edged towards it until he could see outside. The bartender was on one knee in front of the building, a bolt-action rifle aimed directly at the doorway. The girls were scattering towards the outbuildings and Angel heard the beat of hoofs behind the house.

He cursed aloud and then whirled as he heard the scrabble of boots on the floor behind him. A man came up from behind the overturned table across the room. There was a huge bloodstain beneath his left arm, coating his entire body from armpit to waist. He lurched drunkenly, trying to level the heavy gun in his hand, his eyes squinted tight against the pain in his body.

'Damn you!' the man shouted and pulled the trigger in the same instant that Angel squeezed off his own bullet. He felt the raw burn of white pain across his side as the slug sliced along his ribs and he reeled across the open doorway. The bartender saw him and fired, his bullet whacking through the batwing door and shattering the slats into a thousand flying splinters. Angel, down on one knee, saw the man across the room slide forward on his face to the floor, the gun spilling from his nerveless hands. The bartender came running forward across the yard and Angel let him come. The man came flying into the room, the rifle ported ready in his hands and saw Angel in the same moment that Angel laid the barrel of his Army Colt alongside the bartender's head. The man went down hard on his knees and Angel hit him again and then again. The bartender retched, emptying his belly in a pool of stinking vomit as he slid into unconsciousness.

There was an acrid stink of cordite in the air, and the slight breeze through the doorway swung the smoke as if it were tangible. Angel walked out into the sunlight.

He saw the white faces of the girls peering through the window of the outhouse and then the two teamsters who had been drinking earlier at the bar came out into the open. They came warily across the yard as the girls came out, fear in every movement they made.

'Jesus, mister,' one of the teamsters said. 'Jesus.'

'Get those girls over here,' Angel said brusquely. 'I want to know who those men are. Or were.'

The teamsters looked at him thunderstruck.

'Mister, you shot them fellers down an' you don't know who they were?'

Angel nodded. 'One of them was called Juba,' he said. 'The other one is one of the Torellis. I don't know which one.'

'Hell, that's easy, mister,' the teamster said. 'You musta cut down Steve Torelli, 'cause Frank was the one lit out of here like his ass was afire.'

'That's right, mister,' the second man said. They followed Angel into the building, their eyes widening at the havoc. One of them went over and looked down at the man behind the bar. He turned away, his face white and sick.

'Denny Juba,' Angel said. He turned as the girl Carmen came downstairs into the room. 'That right?'

She nodded. Her lips were a thin and bloodless line and now he saw how young she really was.

'Him over there?'

'That's – that was Steve Torelli,' she whispered. 'He – they made me do it, they—'

'Forget it,' he told her. 'It figured they'd try to whip-saw me.'

The girl nodded. 'What about him?' she said, nodding towards the bartender, who was trying to sit up, groaning and holding his bloody head. Angel smiled grimly.

He went across the room and yanked the man to his feet. The bartender cringed away, his face a sweaty mask of fear. 'You know any reason why I should let you stay alive?' Angel asked him. His voice was level and quite normal. He spoke in the tone of a man asking a reasonable question. The bartender gulped and struggled to speak.

'Uh – I—'

'—you tried to cut me down with that,' Angel said, gesturing towards the rifle on the floor. 'That means you're my meat. Unless—'

'—listen, mister,' the bartender gasped. 'I'll do anything. Listen—'

'You listen!' Angel snapped. 'Your life's worth exactly what the next information you give me is worth. Where will Frank Torelli have gone?'

The bartender's face fell.

'Jesus, mister, he'll kill me if I tell you that!' he ejaculated.

'An' I'll kill you if you don't!' Angel said. 'So you don't have a hell of a choice. Except that I'll kill you now. You might have a chance to get some miles between you an' Torelli – always supposing he'd come back here.'

'But, mister, listen—'

'Talk, damn you!' Angel said. 'We're wasting time!'

'He – he might have headed for Mesilla,' the bartender managed. 'He might—'

'This is your last chance, my friend,' Angel said. His voice had lost its edge now and he was calm. The very quietness of his tone frightened the bartender more than anything that had happened this far. He went a fish-belly white and his eyes rolled up in his head as Angel thumbed back the hammer of the Army Colt and placed the barrel to the man's temple.

'Lordsburg!' he screamed. 'He'll head for Cravetts' place in Lordsburg!'

'Are all of them there?'

'I guess so, mister,' the bartender sobbed. 'They left

two days ago. Headin' south. It has to be Lordsburg.'

'It better be,' Angel said. 'Or I'll come looking for you.' He pushed the man away from him and the bartender reeled back against the wall. He felt his way with shaking hands to a table, where he sat down heavily, head in hands, sobbing quietly. Angel looked around at the wrecked saloon. He reached into his pocket and pulled out two gold eagles, tossing them on the blood-stained counter.

'Bury them,' he said.

TWELVE

They were waiting for him in Silver City.

Torelli had run like a rabbit, fear forcing him to the limits of his own endurance on the long, punishing run south and west across the mountains. His mind blank with fear, Torelli thought only of catching up with Cravetts. Cravetts would know what to do. Cravetts would know how to handle this cold-eyed nemesis. Cravetts would tell him who Angel was, why he was on their back-trail, why he wanted to kill them. Still, every jolting racking mile of the way Torelli scoured the dark alleys of his memory for some clue to Angel's identity. Who was he? What did he want? Why did he want him, Torelli, dead?

It did not take long to find his friends in Silver City. They had taken rooms at Antrim's Boarding House on the end of the bridge over the Big Ditch, and were drinking around a table in the Southern Hotel. It took him even less time to tell them what had happened and why he was here.

'He'll come after you?' Cravetts asked.

'Sure as you're born,' Torelli said. 'He's a-crazy!'

'Angel,' Cravetts mused. 'Angel. The name doesn't mean anything to me. Any of you others?'

Lee Monsher shook his head, tow hair falling into his eyes.

81

'Hit ain't the kind o' name a man'd forget,' he said. 'Johnny?'

'I'm never heard of him,' Vister replied. His accent still hinted of his Scandinavian origins. He was a burly man with a broken nose that gave him a good-natured, hell-for-leather look.

'Then who the hell is he?' Torelli ground out. 'Why would he come after us like that?'

Cravetts frowned. 'We've got a long backtrail, Frank,' he said gently. 'Could be something you did, forgot. You say he's young?'

Torelli nodded. 'Nineteen, twenty mebbe.'

'Then he's not Army, he's not Pinkerton, and he's probably – no: he can't be any kind of law. You said he came in and said he was going to kill you, right?' Again Torelli nodded. 'No lawman would ever do that,' Cravetts said. 'Which means he's dogging you for something personal.'

'But I never done nothin' – nothin' that'd make a man track me down like that, Dick! How'd he know where I was? Apart from the boys at the ranch, everyone else thought I was still up in Kansas.'

Cravetts' eyes narrowed.

'He could be from up there. He could be from anywhere. It doesn't make a hell of a lot of difference, Frank.'

'Yo're raht,' Monsher said. 'Hit don't make no sense whichever way you look at it.'

'There's a key,' Cravetts said. 'We just haven't found it.'

'Damned if ah figger to set here a-worryin',' Monsher said. 'Ah'd as lief lay for him an' blow his head off the minnit he shows his face.'

'Oh, we'll do that, all right,' Cravetts said. There was a slow smile on his face. 'No sweat at all. It would just be nice to know what he's after.'

'We'll ask him,' Monsher grinned evilly. 'Just afore we put his light out.'

They laughed uproariously and ordered more drinks, and then they sat down to plan exactly how they were going to whipsaw Frank Angel.

Angel got to Silver City late in the afternoon of the day following Torelli's arrival. Climbing in long loops over the crest of the Black Range, the ten thousand feet of Hillsboro Peak looming up to the north, he dropped down from Emory Pass into the canyons and mountain trails to Santa Rita with its huge opencast copper pit and on into Silver City's Main Street. The clamour and bustle of the place were enormous. Huge freight wagons with teams of a dozen oxen churned the street dust twenty feet high, coating the one- and two-storey business buildings with an overall cast of grey. Up on Chloride Flats above the town the constant chatter of mining machinery throbbed against the empty desert sky. As he came up the street he passed an express office and saw stacks of numbered bricks of silver on the sidewalk outside, unguarded. He checked off the names of the places he would call in on later: the Red Onion, the Blue Goose, the Southern Hotel, the Bullard House. They were all bursting with people: miners, freighters, teamsters, soldiers from Camp Grant and Fort Union, drifting punchers trying their luck in the mines, even a few surly tame Apaches loitering around the entrances to the drinking halls, hoping for a handout. Angel let his eyes drift easily across the faces on the crowded sidewalks, not looking for anyone particular, hoping always to see a face he knew, or would recognise. There wasn't much chance Torelli would be here, but he would check it out. He left his horse in a corral at the edge of town and walked back up the street, wrinkling his nose in disgust at his own smell. A bath, a shave, a change of clothing would be a good idea, too, he thought. Loosening the Army Colt in its holster he set out purposefully to scout the saloons and hotels he had checked off earlier in his mind. A burly man with a broken nose got up off a chair in the shade of the porch outside the Star Hotel as Angel went past, falling in step behind him on the crowded sidewalk. A little further up the street there was a gap between two buildings. Behind it lay a jumble of tipped rubbish and an empty lot stretching back to a pile of tailings looking like a landslide on the bare slope reaching up towards Chloride Flats. Behind Angel the man with the broken nose pulled a handkerchief from his pocket and mopped his face ostentatiously. Then they let the dog see the rabbit. Torelli came out of the Red Onion saloon and walked towards Angel, timing it so that he reached the gap between the buildings at the same moment that Angel saw him. He let Angel's eyes meet his and then gave a yelp of fear, turning on his heel and running flat out up the alley, scrambling over the rubbish and off towards a gully that ran down towards San Vicente creek. There was some scrub and sage down there, but the only cover was a pile of raw timber that had been freighted in and dumped temporarily at the rear of one of the stores. Torelli ran towards it as Angel came pounding up the alley after him, the Army Colt up and out in his hand. He saw Torelli duck behind the lumber pile and hastily threw a shot at the man. The bullet tore a huge sliver of pine from one of the planks and Torelli pulled his own gun and fired back. His bullet whined off way above Angel's head and Angel smiled grimly, running crouched low across the space between him and the pile of timber, eyes fixed on the place he had seen Torelli last, oblivious to everything else. He was about four yards from the timber when two men he had never seen before stepped out into the open. One of them was a lanky man with tow hair that flopped into his eyes and the other was older, thickset, his shoulders broad and heavy, the bull neck corded with anticipation. They had guns in their hands and the guns were fully cocked. Angel skidded to a stop, steeling in a wary crouch. He knew who they were.

'So this is our little Angel,' the man with the tow hair said. There was a feral grin on his face. 'Howdy, Angel. You lookin' for someone?'

Angel said nothing. Looking into those eyes, he knew he was very close to death. There was nothing he could do but the best he could. In another second, another minute he would be dead. It was only a question of whether he could take Cravetts before he went. A flicker of movement to his left caught his eye, and he saw Frank Torelli step out from the other side of the pile of timber, gun ready. Torelli's face was a mask of hatred.

He felt, rather than heard, the slight sound and let the hammer of the gun go, firing even as Vister, coming up behind him, smashed him to the ground with the barrel of his sixgun.

Angel's bullet had been meant for Cravetts but it went a long way wide. He was down on his knees, fighting to stay conscious, knowing that they were coming at him. The gun lay on the ground in front of him. His eyes focused momentarily and he tried to pick the gun up. A boot stomped down on his hand and he felt the raw red flame of pain as the bones went. Then he was yanked to his feet and thrown back against the pile of lumber, jarring the breath from his body.

'Let me!' he heard a voice yell. 'I owe him this!'

'Wait!' another voice said. It had a tone of command, a sureness that it would be obeyed. Cravetts, he thought.

'Hold him,' the same voice said. Rough hands propped him upright. He tried to will strength into his legs but they would not take his weight. There was a long roaring sound in his head, like the sound a train makes in a tunnel.

'Who are you, boy?' Cravetts rasped.

Angel shook his head, wincing at the pain.

'Why you doggin' Torelli, heah?' another voice interjected.

Angel started to shake his head again when Cravetts hit him in the belly. They held him while he retched like a gutshot dog, faces like stone. There was a terrible mushrooming agony in Angel's body and he could not breathe.

'Answer, boy!' the voice said. It came from a long way away. He tried to shake his head. This time the blow was to the face. He knew it because there was the feeling of an explosion, but his brain was not linked to the feeling and there was no pain, just a dull astonished feeling of knowledge that he must be badly hurt. The four men looked at him. Cravetts was splattered with blood from Angel's smashed face. He looked at the others.

'Let me,' Torelli begged. 'Let me at the sonofabitch!'

Cravetts shrugged and stepped aside and Torelli came and stood in front of the sagging wreck that was Angel. He lifted the broken face with a grimy forefinger.

'Angel,' he hissed. 'You hear me?' When Angel did not reply, Torelli slapped his face as hard as he could, then repeated the question. He kept on doing it for perhaps five minutes, his blows tearing the skin off the defenceless man's face, his inexorable questions boring into the dark where that tiny flicker of consciousness left to Angel lay hiding. Angel groaned and tried to nod.

'Who sent you after me, Angel?' Torelli screeched.

There was no way Angel could reply. He wanted to tell them. He would have told them anything if only to stop the awful hurt that was happening inside him. He wanted to tell them about the Gibbons ranch and Sharp and Kamins in the darkened street in Las Vegas, he wanted to tell them all of it but the question he could hear like a thin singing somewhere on the far side of his mind had no answer, for nobody had sent him. He tried to say it, tried to tell the man that nobody had sent him but it came out as 'no', the only syllable the smashed mouth could form.

The refusal drove Torrelli past the point of no return. He drew back, then drove his fist with every ounce of strength he had into the sagging Angel's belly. This time Angel felt something different, something slipping sweet and loose inside him like an oiled bearing, shifting to another place that felt vague and wrong. Blood came out of his gaping mouth and the two men holding him let him go, startled. Angel slumped to the ground and Torelli kicked him and kicked him once more, savagely and punishingly. There were only the faintest flickers of awareness in the cringing thing on the ground now, but it tried to squirm away from the punishment, a ragged wheezing sound coming from it. Angel could only just think now and what he was thinking was that this was dying, that you just went over into the dark without a chance. He did not feel the pain any more, and he did not know when Cravetts finally stopped Torelli.

'That's enough,' the big man said.

'You – you – ain't gonna – leave him?' Torelli panted.

'He's finished,' Cravetts said shortly. 'Why not?'

Torelli shook his head. 'No, Dick,' he said. 'No. No. Finish him off. I'm going to.'

'All right,' Cravetts said. 'But strip him, clean him out good. Not a thing on him to show who he is, you understand? We don't want any posse on our tail when we hit out for Lordsburg.'

'You still aimin' there, Dick?' Monsher said.

Cravetts nodded. 'We pick up Milt and Howie,' he said. 'Then we head for California. That was the plan, and I'm sticking to it.'

'You don't figger mebbe this one—' Monsher jerked his head at the terribly still form of Angel '—told anyone else about us?'

Cravetts shook his head.

'A loner,' he said flatly. 'Like Torelli said, a crazy. He'd never tell anyone anything.'

Monsher nodded. 'I'll buy that,' he said. 'Johnnie?'

Vister nodded his own agreement with their assessment.

'Let's get away from here,' Cravetts said harshly. Then he turned to Frank Torelli, who was standing looking down at the broken, bleeding thing on the ground that was Frank Angel.

'He's all yours,' Cravetts said.

THIRTEEN

Jerry Bigg was drunk.

He got drunk regularly once a month in the Red Onion, part of the reward he paid himself for grovelling in the dirt like a gopher, for thirty days placering up in the Burro Mountains. He had a set routine. A bath and a shave, a room at the Star Hotel, where Del Truesdell would look after Jerry's dust while he had what he called his 'whoopdang-dingle'; a couple of drinks with the steak and egg and canned tomatoes he would eat before spending some time at Morrill's Opera House, watching the show, giving the girls the eye; and then some serious drinking at the saloon. Jerry was a 'quiet' drinker, never gave anybody any trouble. Harvey Whitehill, the sheriff, knew him and let him alone, even when Jerry started singing songs about his mother in a terrible off-key tenor.

So here it was getting towards midnight and Jerry was well and truly smashed. He had his arm around one of the Red Onion's bar-girls, a pert little redhead called Jenny who was stringing the miner along for all the drinks she could get out of him. The girls in the place had a rota system with Jerry, which was the only fair way to play it. He was openhanded to the point of stupidity when he was having his sprees, and he had never laid a hurtful hand on anyone of them, which was no small blessing if you worked in the Red Onion.

' 's oft in the cool of the eeeeeeeeevenin,' Jerry was roaring softly, his voice full of maudlin passion, 'whe' the shadders shink in th' west . . .'

'Come on, honey,' Jenny told him. 'Knock off on that yowlin', will ya?'

'Yowlin'?' Jerry said owlishly. 'Shin – singin', that is. "I think o' the twi-hi-ligh' song you shang, an' the boy you loved the best . . ." '

'Aw, c'mon, honey,' the girl said, wriggling herself around against him. 'Don't ya wanna come back to my place?'

He looked at her, drawing his head back and focusing on the painted pouting little face. 'Wharra pretty gal,' he remarked.

'We could get a bottle an' go back to my place, Jerry,' the girl said. 'Wouldn'tcha like that?'

'Madam,' Bigg said, staggering to his feet and almost spilling the girl to the floor, 'your servant. Wharra pretty girl,' he said to a smiling crowd of miners at the next table.

One of them neighed like a horse and there was a burst of laughter. Jerry Bigg glared at them for a moment, then his natural good humour reasserted itself.

'Bringa bottle,' he told the girl and headed for the door. She caught him as he veered off towards the right, his balance centres totally out of kilter, grimacing at one of the other girls by the bar.

'Good luck, honey,' the other girl minced.

'Up yours,' said Jenny elegantly, and lurched out into the crowded street with Jerry Bigg leaning heavily on her. People made room for them on the sidewalk, grinning hugely as Jerry burst brokenly into song as they reeled along. She piloted him up the street and turned left into the alleyway towards her shack on Sandy Lane. She figured Jerry still had twenty or thirty dollars left and saw no earthly reason why he should waste it on the Red Onion's rotgut, good money that she could nicely use. She had a sock inside her mattress with a hundred and twenty dollars saved already and when she had enough she was going to open a place of her own and then, by God! let any horny-handed bastard try to lay a finger on her! She staggered down the alley with Jerry still singing happily, waving the bottle he was clutching firmly by the neck. If she could get him into bed, he'd go out like a light and wouldn't remember tomorrow whether he'd spent the money on drink or her or both. Perspiration streaked her heavy makeup and she cursed silently as she helped the drunken miner down the side of a shallow gully that ran behind the Orpheum. Her place was on the far side. Jerry stumbled and slid down into the wash on his backside. She let him go and then went down into the brush-choked gully where Bigg was pawing around like a drowning swimmer, laughing uproariously at this new pastime. As she hitched up her skirts and eased down the slope, Jenny saw a white thing lying off behind the bushes. She thought at first it was an old mattress, or some discarded pottery, for the light was poor. Frowning she took a step towards it and then saw it was the body of a naked man and as the moon soared clear of the cloud for a moment she saw what had been done to it and started screaming. Jerry Bigg froze as the scream rent the air and then tried to get to his feet, falling over in his haste and panic.

Jenny kept on screaming until the sheriff came pounding down into the gully and followed her pointing

91

finger to the naked body of Frank Angel. The girl stopped screaming then and started sobbing as they shepherded her away. She had no idea at all that she had saved a man's life.

FOURTEEN

Angus Wells heard about Angel in Mesilla.

The two teamsters who had been at Torelli's road ranch when Angel had come there had brought the story of what happened with them, and it was still very much gossip fodder. The bartender in the *cantina* opposite the Wells Fargo office was only too happy to tell the story again for the benefit of a stranger in town, and as he listened, Wells decided to play a hunch. Years of working for the Department of Justice had taught him the wisdom of following the 'feel' that you got from such a story rather than its bald facts, and there was a feel to this one which he could almost touch with his hands. Angel! He recalled his conversation with the Attorney-General in the high-ceilinged room in Washington. There was no question in his mind now that the boy who had been a hired hand on the Gibbons ranch had somehow, miraculously, traced the raiders and tracked them all the way from Kansas, wreaking bloody vengeance in Torelli's place. Nor was there any question in his mind that the boy would go on after Torelli, oblivious of or unheeding of the fact that now the hunted would become the hunter. Angel had played lucky, for his quarry had not known he was their pursuer. But now the tables would be turned and they would be waiting for him. In his mind, as the bartender droned on, repeating with relish details which got bloodier at every recounting, Wells unrolled the map of New Mexico in his head. Down the valley of the Rio Grande, as far as Animas Peak, so would a fleeing man ride, turning up into the mountains and towards Silver City, then down through the pine-clad fastness of the Burro Mountains towards Lordsburg – for now the information Wells had gathered in Lincoln came together with the trace that Angel must have blazed across the west. The tangents would meet at Lordsburg, Wells knew. But the proof would be in Silver City. If there was a man there called Angel – dead, or alive – then Wells would know where Cravetts and his raiders were, too. Angel alive – they were coming. Angel dead – they would be in Lordsburg.

The bartender was sorry to see him go: it wasn't often he had such an attentive and appreciative audience, and he heaved a sigh and went back to polishing the row of glasses behind his bar.

Wells got the whole story from the sheriff in Silver City.

Harvey Whitehill's office was on the south side of Main, a one-storey building next to a Chinese laundry. Inside there was a large room running the depth of the building, divided by a low wooden railing such as you sometimes saw in eastern police stations. Behind it there were two desks, some cupboards, a chained and padlocked rifle rack containing several riot guns, and behind them a solid adobe wall into which were set heavy barred doors.

The sheriff was a softly-spoken man with a drooping walrus moustache and a deliberate, gentle air. His bushy eyebrows climbed a fraction when Wells produced his credentials and asked his questions.

'Department of Justice?' he said, tapping his teeth

with a pencil. 'That's high-powered stuff to be interesed in an alley-fight.'

'You had one, then?'

Whitehill nodded. 'Kid by the name of Angel, would you believe it? He was found in a gully by one of the girls from the Red Onion – that's a saloon down the street – takin' a miner home with her. He was in bad shape.'

'Was?'

Whitehill nodded. 'Looks like he'll pull through,' he said. 'No thanks to the men who fixed his wagon, though.'

'Any indication what happened?'

'I spoke to the boy when he came round,' Whitehill told him. 'He was pretty tightlipped about the whole thing. Wouldn't give me too much detail, but I did some scouting around, pieced it all together.'

Wells started to roll a cigarette, offered the cotton sack of Bull Durham to the sheriff. Whitehill shook his head.

'Tryin' to give it up,' he said. 'Don't know as I'll do her, though. Well, sir, what I figure happened was three or four fellers took that bitty kid out behind a pile o' lumber there an' beat him within an inch of his life. Then someone who knew exactly what he was doin' started in on kickin' what was left o' the life out of him. Then he was stripped naked an' tossed into the gully where he was found. Whoever done it probably figgered the kid was dead already but just to make sure he put a few bullets into him. One through the belly and one through each leg.'

Despite himself, Wells shuddered. He told Whitehill about the raid on the Gibbons farm, the robbery of the Army payroll, Angel's pursuit of the seven men, the fight at Torelli's, all of it.

'Shoot,' Whitehill said. 'Hardly seems possible. That boy can't be more than twenty.'

'He did it,' Wells told him. 'Believe me.'

'No wonder they done that to him, then,' Whitehill said, tapping his teeth again with the pencil. 'It'd be by way of warnin' anyone else who had a mind to follow them that it was a poor idea.' He let his eyes rest squarely on Wells.

'Can I see the boy?' Wells asked.

'Sure, I can fix that,' Whitehill said. 'You goin' after them fellers?'

Wells nodded grimly. 'I know where they'll be heading,' he said. 'But maybe you can help me some. Ask around. Someone must have seen them here. I'll give you a list of the names. I need descriptions: what they were wearing, whether they had beards or not, what kind of horses they were riding, whether—'

'I think I can guess the kind of thing you'll want,' Whitehill said drily. 'I'll take you over to the Southern, an' then do some askin' round. You want to look in here later?'

They got up and walked together down the street to the two-storey brick building with the big wooden sign nailed to the railed gallery on the first floor. Whitehill nodded to the desk clerk and led the way to a room at the back of the hotel, and went in. Wells followed, getting his first look at Frank Angel.

The boy's face was puffed and swollen, huge black bruises marking the area from his eyebrows to his jawbone. His right hand was swathed in bandages, and Wells could see more bandages crisscrossing the lower part of the chest. Angel watched them come in with eyes both expressionless and wary.

'Son, this here is Mr Wells, wants to ask you a few questions,' the sheriff said. 'You feel like talkin' any?'

Angel said nothing. Wells looked at Whitehill who shrugged, and then turned and went out of the room.

Wells looked around and found a chair, which he pulled alongside the bed.

'So you're Frank Angel,' he said.

Angel lowered his eyelids in acknowledgement.

'My name is Angus Wells, son,' Wells said. 'I'm a lawman. Want to show you something.'

He reached into his pocket and brought out a badge. It was circular and at its centre was the screaming eagle of the United States. Around the border were the words 'Department of Justice, United States of America'. Wells held it where Angel could see it.

'I'm what the Department of Justice calls a Special Investigator, Frank,' he said. He smiled humourlessly. 'Senior Special Investigator, actually. I'm acting under direct orders from the Attorney-General of the USA. You understand?' Again the slow movement of the eyelids. Nothing more.

'Now you and I seem to be looking for the same people, son, even if we have different reasons,' Wells went on. 'I want Cravetts and his raiders because they robbed an Army payroll, as well as for what they did at the Gibbons place. If we can arrest them, they'll hang, every man jack of them. But I need all the help I can get tracking them down. How about telling me what you know?'

'Arrest?' The word came from the split, swollen lips as if it had been pulled out with pliers.

'It says Department of Justice on the badge, son,' Wells said gently. 'Not Department of Revenge.'

'My way better,' Angel said.

Wells shook his head. 'No it isn't, boy, and I'll tell you why. You may think you have the best reasons in the world for tracking down Cravetts and his bunch and killing them like the animals they undoubtedly are, but you're forgetting something. By killing them you are placing yourself in grave danger of becoming as much a murderer as any of them. Even if what happened to you' – he nodded at the bandages – 'wasn't warning enough that you're not equipped to handle men like these.'

'Doin' all right,' mumbled Angel.

'When you had surprise on your side, boy,' snapped Wells. 'When they didn't know you were after them! But now they know your face. You come within twenty yards of them again and you'll be dead. Goddammit! You're lucky to be alive as it is!'

'Tough on them,' the boy in the bed said. 'Mistake they'll regret.'

Wells looked at him as if he had gone completely mad.

'Are you telling me you're going to go after them again?' he said.

Angel gave the assent sign with his eyelids.

Wells let his breath out in an exasperated rush.

'Have you got any idea how bad hurt you were?' he said, regretting his words the moment he had said them and saw the flurry of pain and panic come into the younger man's eyes.

'Son,' Wells said gently, 'you won't be able to ride for a month or more. Maybe not even then. By that time Cravetts and his men will be long gone. You can't start out on a cold trail again. Leave off now. You've done more than anyone could have expected of you. Juba's dead, so that's one less for me to worry about. And—'

'Two more,' Angel said. 'Sharp and Kamins.'

'Wha – what about Sharp and Kamins?' Wells said, sharply.

'Dead,' Angel said. 'Killed them. Las Vegas.'

'You killed Milt Sharp and Howie Kamins?' Wells said in astonished voice. 'How? – did you bushwack them?' Angel moved his head slightly from side to side.

'You took on two of the best guns in the Territory and

came out alive? Listen, son—'

'It's true.' There was such finality in Angel's voice that Wells stilled his own outburst. It could be possible. It was unbelievable but it could be possible. The element of surprise. . . .

'You used a gun much?' he said, artlessly, changing the subject. Angel made the head-shaking movement again.

'Know anything about gunfighting? Snapshooting? Fast draw?'

Again the headshake.

'Blind luck!' Wells said, flatly. 'You ran in blind luck. You took on casehardened gunmen and came out of it alive because you were a fool for luck, Angel! The minute you were out there on your own and they knew you for who you were, your luck ran out. And they cut you up like a side of beef!' He stood up, gesturing contemptuously at the figure in the bed. 'Look at yourself!' he said. 'You think you're in any kind of shape to take on these men? Christ, boy, they'd eat you for breakfast and look around for seconds!'

Angel had turned his head away. Wells stopped, suddenly embarrassed at his own vehemence. He thought he could see the glint of tears in the boy's eyes.

'Well, haarrumph! Well, now,' he said, sitting down again. 'Didn't mean to be hard on you, son. But catching men like these is for pros. You tell me about them. Anything you can. What they look like. How they talk. Dress, anything. I'll track them on down to Lordsburg. That's where they'll be. Then I'll take them. Listen: with your help or without it, I'm going after them: You help me, it'll be that much easier. But I'm going anyway, son. That's my job.'

Angel had turned over in the bed and Wells saw he had been listening carefully. He didn't say anything more, just sat waiting.

There were a long couple of minutes of silence, and then Angel started to talk. He told Wells about the Gibbons ranch, and what had happened and then he told him the rest. He talked as long as he could, his throat working sometimes to keep back the tears of anger at his own stupidity, described what he could remember about the night he had gone running up the alley after Torelli. Towards the end, his voice started to drift a little, and when he had finished, he was asleep in an instant, exhausted. Wells stood up, looking down at the battered face. He let himself quietly out of the room and went back across the street to Whitehill's office.

The sheriff looked up, his curiosity plain on his face.

'That's quite a boy,' he said. 'Quite a boy.'

Whitehill nodded. 'Must have the constitution of an ox to still be alive,' he confirmed. 'What they did to him would've killed many a grown man.'

Wells sat down in the chair opposite the sheriff's desk. He told him briefly most – but not all – of what Angel had said, and then asked Whitehill if he had learned anything. Whitehill nodded.

'Four o' them, there was,' he said. 'Someone remembered them in the Orpheum drinking. Once I had the names it wasn't hard. They was three at first: they took rooms with Katy Antrim down the end of the street. Her boy Henry remembered them – smart youngster. Gave me some useful stuff. What they were wearing, like that. The fourth one came the day after them. They left town the night the Angel kid was – beaten up. Took the Lordsburg road.' He picked up the pencil, tapping his teeth with it. 'You going after them?' he asked.

'I could use some help,' Wells said quietly.

'Like to give it,' Whitehill said, his face serious, 'but Lordsburg ain't my bailiwick, Wells. I got no authority outside of Grant County.'

'The United States Marshal is at Santa Fé,' Wells reminded him quietly.

'I know it,' Whitehill said. 'I could come down there with you – unofficial-like, if you've a mind.'

Wells shook his head. 'No,' he said slowly. 'I'm beholden to you for offering. It wouldn't look good for you if we caught up with them and you were involved – unofficial-like.' He smiled to take any offence from the words.

'What you want me to do?' Whitehill asked.

'You could get a telegraph message through for me to Washington,' Wells told him. 'If any of our people are in this part of the world, maybe they can get word to them. Have them send a reply to Lordsburg.'

'Easy done,' Whitehill said. 'Anything else?'

'The kid,' Wells said. 'What'll happen to him?'

Whitehill shrugged. 'He'll have to work some to pay off his doctor bills – when he can,' he said.

'Send him back home,' Wells said. 'Don't let him come after me.'

He opened his money-belt and pulled out some notes.

'A hundred and fifty,' he said. 'If there's anything over, give it to the kid for clothes. Then put him on a train and send him back to Kansas. OK?'

'OK with me,' Whitehill said heavily. 'You checked with him?'

'He'll do it,' Wells said. 'He hasn't any choice at all.'

'I'll tell him you said that,' Whitehill smiled.

'Tell him I meant it, too,' was the unsmiling reply.

FIFTEEN

Wells overplayed his hand.

Lordsburg was a long straggling collection of adobes and one-storey frame buildings stretching along the main trail from Las Cruces to Tucson with its road forking at the western edge of town up towards the mining towns of Safford and Globe. When he got in, Wells went directly to the telegraph office. Identifying himself, he was given a telegraph message from Washington, which he broke open there and then and read, cursing. No personnel from the Justice Department in this area. He went to the counter and asked the clerk for some paper, writing a message to the Commanding Officer at Fort Bowie in Arizona. It was succinct and peremptory. NEED MILITARY ASSISTANCE ARREST OUTLAWS RESPONSIBLE ARMY PAYROLL ROBBERY KANSAS STOP WANTED MEN HERE IN LORDSBURG TELEGRAPH REPLY IMMEDIATELY STOP

'Sign it Wells, Department of Justice,' he told the clerk who looked at him goggle-eyed, his mouth open. 'I'll wait for the reply.' He sat down on the hard bench that ran across one of the walls and fanned himself with his Stetson. It was as hot as the hinges of hell outside, and inside the cluttered little shack which housed the telegraph office the temperature was near to the hundred

102

mark. He listened to the stuttering metallic chatter of the telegrapher's key and imagined the wires loping across the long empty spaces, under the shadow of the Dos Cabezas, through the vicious lonely territory of the Chiricahua Apaches to the heat-blasted hell-hole in the very foothills of Cochise's old stronghold – Fort Bowie. He rolled a cigarette and smoked it. Later he smoked another, and was halfway through it when the telegrapher's key started chattering again. He got up quickly, crushing out the cigarette on the earthen floor, and waited impatiently as the clerk wrote down the message. When the man came across to the counter Wells snatched the paper from him and scanned it eagerly. Then he crumpled it into a ball and threw it at the wall, giving vent to a muted oath.

Its words lingered in his mind's eye, mocking him. REGRET IMPOSSIBLE DETACH PATROL ASSIST YOU DUE RECENT OUTBREAK APACHES STOP ALL AVAILABLE MEN AT FULL READINESS HOSTILITIES STOP GOOD LUCK STOP

It had been signed by the Commanding Officer of the Fort.

Wells turned to the clerk.

'Where can I get a room?' he asked.

'Ho-tel's up the street a couple o' blocks, Mister Wells,' the clerk said. 'Turn right as you leave.'

He watched the tall lawman leave and then scuttled around the counter and picked up the crumpled piece of paper Wells had left on the floor. Crossing quickly to the door, he checked that Wells was indeed on his way to the hotel, and then ran back to his desk, switching off the machine. He let himself out of the back door of the telegraph office and ran up the alley until he came to the adobe wall which stood behind the hardware store. There was a gate in the wall, through which he let

103

himself, running up to the back door of the store and into its cool darkness.

'Johnny here?' he asked the slatternly woman behind the counter. She looked up and nodded. 'He's aroun' heah someplace,' she said listlessly, then screamed 'Johnnneeeee!' Several screams later a freckle-faced lad of about twelve poked his head warily around the screen door and said 'Huh?'

The clerk beckoned him forward and pushed a silver dollar into his hand. 'You get on your pony an' ride out to the Cravetts place with this note, son,' he said. 'You tell Mr Cravetts I sent you an' he's to give you another dollar.'

The boy looked at him with wide eyes. 'Two whole dollars?' he said.

'Get goin' now, boy,' the clerk said. He watched anxiously as the boy ran out to the corral alongside the building and threw a saddle and blanket on the pinto standing in the shade. The boy whirled off in a cloud of dust, heading southeast as straight as an arrow, and the telegraph clerk watched him go and then slowly smiled, the anxiety lifting from his shoulders. Dick Cravetts was the biggest rancher in these parts, and he had made an arrangement some time ago with the telegraph clerk that anything of especial interest going across the wires should be passed on to him. He said it helped him with his business, and the clerk figured it must, since every time he had passed on items of information, Cravetts had given him twenty dollars, one time fifty. This Justice Department business would be worth another gold eagle sure, the telegraph clerk told himself. He walked back to his office with a wide smile on his face, tipping his derby to two women shopping in the street.

They gave Wells absolutely no chance at all.

He was in a *cantina* on the east end of town when the four men came in out of the night. Two of them sat at a table, and the other two went to the bar, one on each side of Wells. He did not notice them at first, for the place was crowded and noisy, but eventually he looked up and saw the man along the bar on his right. The tow hair gleamed dull gold in the lamplight and the man grinned at Wells and raised his shot glass in a mock salute. Wells checked to the left, where he saw a big man with a broken nose standing, left arm on the bar, right hand hanging loose near a holstered sixgun. He cursed himself silently for his own stupidity, his mind racing to find a way of giving himself any kind of a fighting chance. He turned around slowly and then his heart sank completely. At a table in front of him was sitting a man who could only be, from the description that Wells knew by heart, Dick Cravetts. He smiled, showing fine strong white teeth.

'Mr Wells,' he said. 'Understand you're looking for me.'

His voice was hardly raised and yet everyone in the place heard what he said. The phrase was in no way unusual, and yet within fifteen seconds the room was cleared, with everyone who had been in there outside on the sidewalk, craning to see through the windows and over the top of the batwing doors.

'You're Cravetts?' Wells said.

Cravetts nodded. 'On my left, here, Frank Torelli. By the bar, on your right Johnnie Vister; on the other side Lee Monsher.'

Wells nodded. 'The telegrapher?' he asked.

'Right first time,' Cravetts said. He lifted the hand that had been concealed beneath the table and showed Wells the Navy Colt held in it.

'Not even a fighting chance?' Wells said. He was

105

breathing very softly, tensing up slowly for the next thing he was going to have to do.

'Not even,' Cravetts said and eared back the hammer. In that moment Wells went up on his toes and over the bar backwards. He was in peak condition and trained to a hair, and his movement startled Cravetts enough to fire hastily. The .36 calibre slug hit Wells' right hip as he flipped backwards on his shoulders and whacked his body around so that he fell in a sprawling heap behind the bar, the lower part of his body a tearing mass of pain. Now everything he had learned in fourteen years with the Justice Department came into play and the gun which had already been in his hand even as his back hit the bar came up and boomed into the face of Johnnie Vister as he jumped up on to the bar for a clear shot at the sprawling lawman. Vister's face dissolved into a red smear and he went over backwards in a huge whirling pile, smashing tables and chairs to kindling as his heavy body landed. Cravetts and Torelli were both on their feet moving crabwise across the *cantina* towards the corners of the room and Lee Monsher was on the floor in front of the bar. He gave a thumbs up signal to Cravetts and emptied his gun through the thin timber facings below the heavier bar, spacing the bullets about six inches apart. They tore through the soft wood like butter, and would have cut Wells apart had he been able to move. That he had been badly hit, however, the raiders did not know, and Monsher's shots went wild. Cravetts scuttled for the end of the bar near where Vister's grisly corpse lay and dived full length for the floor, coming around the bar enough to throw a shot behind the bar where he thought Wells might be. The bullet would have taken the lawman about belly height had he been crouching where Cravetts expected him to be, but Wells was still lying on his back and the bullets whined over him. He fired at the flash of Cravett's Navy and his bullet burned a long furrow down the man's back from left shoulder to buttock. Cravetts gave a long scream of pain and rolled out of range cursing as Lee Monsher, his gun reloaded, vaulted over the bar in one smooth sweeping leap. He came down with both heels on Wells' outstretched legs. Wells' head went back against the dirt floor as the terrible pain smashed into his brain and he felt nothing as the tow-haired man kicked the gun out of his hand.

'OK,' Monsher said, standing up.

Cravetts was standing now as well, blood spreading a dark stain across the back of his shirt. He cursed at the pain of movement and snarled 'Bring him around here!'

Monsher and Torelli dragged the half-conscious lawman around the bar and dumped him on the floor. Cravetts picked up a whiskey bottle and poured it on the man's face until he spluttered and tried to sit up.

'Hold the bastard!' he snapped. Monsher and Torelli half lifted Wells upright, while Cravetts slapped his face openhanded and contemptuous, until Wells moaned and opened his eyes. The first thing he saw was the sentence of death written in Cravetts' eyes, and he waited for the shocking pain of the final bullet.

'No,' Cravetts said. He let the rage seep out of his eyes. His iron will was assuming control, straightening him up, cold and pitiless as a warring Apache.

'Lawman,' he said softly.

Monsher and Torelli looked at him and then stepped away. Wells swayed, trying to keep his feet. The pain in his wounded hip was white and intense but he would not let himself go down on the floor again.

'Lawman,' Cravetts repeated. 'I'm going to let you live. But only so that you'll be a living reminder to your Justice Department friends of what will happen if they send anyone else after me.'

'You don't . . . you don't think anything you . . . do to me will stop them, do you?' Wells managed.

'Be interesting to find out,' Cravetts said, and shot Wells through the right thigh. Wells screamed and fell writhing on the floor, blood gouting from the shattered mess of flesh and bone. His hands thrashed on the dirt floor and blood spilled from his mouth where he had bitten right through his tongue. Cravetts laughed and then shot Wells' right hand to bits. There was a terrible silence, for Wells' was unconscious, deep in the blackness of total agony. Gunsmoke swayed in the still air. Torelli and Monsher looked at their leader with white faces.

'We oughta kill him, Dick,' Monsher said.

'No,' Cravetts said softly. 'Let him live. He'll never walk properly again, never use a gun with that hand. He's finished.'

'He knows what we look like,' Torelli said, nervously. 'Who we are.'

'So what?' Cravetts said. His grin was like Satan's death mask. 'Tomorrow we head out for California. No more waiting. Johnnie's gone. Milt an' Howie aren't here and the deadline is past. We split the money three ways and disappear.'

'What about the ranch?' Monsher said.

'Sold, two months back,' Cravetts grinned. 'The money's already in the Cattleman's Bank in San Francisco.'

He looked down at the maimed thing on the *cantina* floor and spat on it.

'*Vamonos!*' he said.

SIXTEEN

In four weeks Angel was well enough to ride.

Although his wounds were by no means fully healed, he worked hard at the job of blanking out the pain until he could adjust to it, live with it, a constant companion which was always there, an old acquaintance whose foibles he knew well. It was an act of will which astonished the old doctor who had cared for him, and which for some reason he could not altogether pin down made Sheriff Harvey Whitehill nervous. He had long before this extracted from the boy a straight-faced promise that when he was better he would head back East for Kansas, forget all this business of trying to catch Cravetts and his raiders. Angel had nodded and agreed with all of Whitehill's conditions, He had gotten himself a part-time job waiting table at the Star Hotel, and when he had saved enough money he went to the livery stable and bought himself a horse. He also bought himself a new Colt's Army model, but he did not tell Whitehill about that, or the soft leather gunbelt in which the gun nestled beneath his bed. Finally the day came when he told Whitehill he was heading out.

'I want you to know how grateful I am to you, Sheriff,' he said, and there was sincerity in the words. Whitehill had heard earlier that Angel had ridden up to the Burros and found Jerry Bigg, taking him two bottles of whiskey which had caused Jerry to miss two whole days' digging. He had also, Whitehill learned, given the dance-hall girl Jenny twenty-five dollars, although Whitehill didn't know that it was all the money Angel had.

'Just you mind what you told me, son,' Whitehill said, tapping his teeth with the pencil. 'You head on home and leave the lawin' to the lawmen.'

Angel nodded, and after a brief handshake swung up into the saddle and headed the horse up the street and on to the trail towards Santa Rita, heading East. Whitehill watched him go and went back into his office, frowning.

'Too damned tame by a mile,' he said to nobody in particular, taking a kick at the leg of his desk. 'Too damned tame by a mile!'

His estimate of Angel's character was perfect. Up in the mountains, where the trail forked to the south towards Hurley, Angel swung his horse's head around and headed steadily on down along the empty arroyo of the San Vicente. About fifteen miles south of Silver City he took a sighting on Burro Peak where it reared above the pineclad shoulders of the mountains, and let the horse make its own pace over the fifteen miles that brought him back to the trail going south and west to Lordsburg. He was there by nightfall, and by dawn he was on his way again, heading now for Fort Bowie, raging with impatience at the slow miles rolling past, the sketchy story of what had happened to Wells in the Lordsburg *cantina* revolving in his mind like a litany. The young cavalry lieutenant who had given him the story in the telegraph office had said that Wells had almost died of his wounds, loss of blood and shock. Yet he had found enough strength to make two Mexicans carry him on a cot down to the telegraph office, where he had arrested the telegraph clerk after forcing him to send a message

110

to Fort Bowie – effecting this by calmly threatening to do to the clerk exactly what had been done to him. A detachment had been sent across from the Fort and Wells had gone back there in an ambulance, while the patrol went out to the Cravetts ranch to search it for any clues as to where the raiders might have gone. What they had found or not found the soldier did not know. Angel knew Army procedure now. The officers at Fort Bowie would know. Whether they would tell him was something else. If Wells was still alive, he might make them. He recalled what Wells had said to him the last time he had seen the lawman, and grimaced. It wasn't likely.

He moved carefully across the empty land, keeping the twin nipples of the Dos Cabezas on his left, eyes always wary for dust or pony sign. Up behind those peaks were the Chiricahua mountains, and enough Apaches in them, no doubt, to double the population at San Simon. Nothing moved in the land of the Apaches that they did not see. He wanted no trouble with them and the best way to ensure that was to stay a long way away from them, hoping they wouldn't consider it worthwhile running down a lone rider. If they felt like doing it, he had about as much chance as a mouse in a cat basket.

Because he could not travel fast, it took Angel until almost nightfall to reach Bowie. The fort sprawled ungainly across the valley, lights in the officers' quarters sparkling bright, visible many miles across the desert in the pure night air. He could hear them sounding retreat as he came over the last high crest and canted down towards the establishment, and the long twilight was almost gone as he came up the long gravelled street behind the quartermaster's building and the post trader's, a long, low adobe with a ramada four feet wide, as dark beneath at night as a cellar. He led his horse to the building a passing soldier told him was the adjutant's office, and inquired there about Wells.

'You a friend of his?' the thickset sergeant behind the desk asked.

'In a way,' Angel said. 'I met him in Silver City.'

'You know what happened to him?'

'Yes,' Angel said. 'A Lieutenant Roward in Lordsburg told me. That's why I came. Can I see him?'

'As to that, I can't say,' the sergeant said heavily. 'It's the doctor you'll have to be askin'. Corporal!'

The door opened smartly and a young corporal, the yellow stripes very bright and fresh on his sleeve, stamped into the room and stood rigidly at attention.

'Take this young gentleman across to the Hospital,' the sergeant said. 'To see Doctor Bowall.'

'Sarge!' the corporal said. 'This way, sir!' he invited Angel, who grinned in the darkness outside.

'Follow me, mister,' the soldier said, and led the way across the baked earth of the parade ground towards a long low building on the southern perimeter. It was brightly lit at every window and as they got closer Angel could see men lying in cots, some reading, others sleeping. In a small office at the end of the hospital, he was introduced to the Post Surgeon, Doctor Bowall. 'Mister Angel,' Bowall acknowledged. 'You say you want to see Wells. May I ask why?'

'He . . . helped me when I was . . . hurt. In Silver City,' Angel said. 'By the same men that . . . did what they did to him.'

'Ah,' the doctor said. 'And did they tell you what that was?'

'I heard they shot him up real bad.'

'That they did, boy,' the doctor nodded, scratching a match against the adobe wall and lighting an evil-looking black stogie. He puffed the smoke out of the doorway into the stillness of the night, watching it hang in the lamplight. 'And more than that.'

'More?'

'Aye, lad, more,' Bowall said flatly. 'You see, they destroyed his pride. They took everything that mattered away from him except his life. And that was more cruel to the man than killing him would have been.'

'I – don't—'

'Understand? No, why would you?' the grizzled old doctor said. His voice was soft and reassuring. He let another stream of smoke drift off into the starlight. 'Medicine's a very inexact business, laddie,' he explained. 'Out here, everything is so – well, primitive. We have no facilities for dealing with anything other than the physical aspects of the business. We fix the bullet wounds, patch up the broken bones, mend the torn flesh. It's about all we can do.'

He sighed, and then patted a chair. 'Sit down, lad, sit down. You look all in.'

Angel sank gratefully into the chair.

'What happened to your friend was this,' Bowall said. 'The men who shot him deliberately crippled him. They shot his leg apart – God knows if he'll ever ride a horse again – and then they put a bullet into his hand so he could never handle a gun. Now you know he's a lawman?'

'Department of Justice Special Investigator,' Angel nodded.

'Just so,' Bowall said. 'Did you know he was their top man? Yes, he's been fourteen years with them. His job was his life. And what they did, you see, was to make it absolutely impossible for him ever to do his job again.

'You mean the wounds won't mend?'

'Oh, they'll mend, lad,' Bowall said, gesturing with the stogie. 'But that's what I meant about how limited what the doctor can do is. For them to mend is one thing. For the man to want to try to be a whole human being again is something else. Your friend Wells simply does not want to live.'

'Why are you telling me all this?' Angel said.

'So you'll help him, help me,' the doctor said. 'I want you to try and get him out of this – this depression. He won't listen to me any more. Or anyone. He is deep in the black depths of thinking he will never be any use to anyone again.'

'But what—?'

'Can you do? I don't know, lad, I don't know. You see, I know about you – yes, he told me. Angel. It's not a name for forgetting easily, now is it? But you and he have one thing in common. This man Cravetts. He won't talk about him to me, not any more. He thinks he has failed completely, in his job, as a man. You're the only one I can think of who might snap him around out of it.'

'Hell, doc, I don't know if I can—'

Bowall laid a hand on Angel's shoulder.

'You say he helped you. Well, maybe you can help him now.'

Angel nodded. 'I'll do what I can,' he said.

Bowall stood up, smiling. 'I hoped you would. I had a feeling in my bones you might turn up. God knows why – by all accounts, anyone with a lick of sense would be on his way home, glad to be alive.'

'I'll go home one day,' Angel said. 'When I've finished what I started out to do.'

There was an intensity in his words which hung in the air, and the doctor frowned. In the lamplight the boy looked no older than his own son. He thought of Laurence, freshfaced and smiling in his cadet's uniform at West Point, and compared him mentally with this youngster with the hard lines of experience already shaping his face. My God, he thought, this bloody country!

114

He opened the door and pointed down the hospital ward. Angel saw Wells in the bed on the right. Wells was sitting upright, his right arm in a wadded, bandaged sling, his right leg splinted and held in traction. He was gazing emptily at the wall opposite his bed and there was no expression on his face when Angel came up beside the bed.

'Wells,' he said, tentatively.

Wells' eyes swung around, widening fractionally as he saw who his visitor was. Then the fleeting expression fled from the eyes and they were empty again.

'They . . . told me what . . . what happened,' Angel said.

Nothing.

'You mad because I broke my word?' Angel asked him.

Again nothing.

'I'm going on after them, Wells,' the boy said.

Wells blinked, blinked again. Angel watched silently in astonishment as two huge tears formed in the older man's eyes and trickled down his unmoving face.

'Go away,' Wells said. His voice was flat and colourless.

'Wells, you've got to help me,' Angel said.

The lawman's head swung around and he fixed baleful, swimming eyes on the boy at his bedside.

'Help!' he said. He made a noise that might have been a contemptuous laugh bisected by a sob. 'Help you! What do I use for a hand? How do I get on a horse? You going to give me one of your legs, boy?'

Angel felt a sudden sureness inside him and it welled up and out and became a laugh, a big laugh that made the soldiers in the other beds turn their heads in astonishment, craning to see the extraordinary sight of the beardless boy laughing by Wells' bed.

'Yes, yes, yes!' Angel said, letting the laugh die back to a wide grin, seeing the tears tremble on Wells' eyelids and slither down his face as Wells looked at him and then smiled and then smiled again.

'You can teach me!' Angel shouted and made no effort to keep the excitement out of his voice. 'You can use my hands, Wells! My legs! Show me, Wells! Teach me!'

Still Wells said nothing, just looked at Angel with an aching uncertainty in his eyes. He shook his head but there was no conviction at all in the gesture.

'You can!' Angel shouted. 'We can! Both of us, Wells! We can!'

The sound of the raised voices brought the doctor hurrying down the length of the hospital, but he stopped short when he saw the look on Wells' face, the eager eyes of the younger man by his bedside. Wells looked up and his eyes met those of the doctor.

'Can I?' he whispered. 'Could I?'

Bowall smiled.

'Angus,' he said. 'You know damned well you could.'

SEVENTEEN

By the time they were ready to move out, the trail was two months old. They had done some backtracking, of course. The Army had made extensive inquiries at Lordsburg, and the telegraph office clerk had been questioned and then questioned again and then again until they were sure they had wrung every ounce of information the man could give them out of him. What they had was pretty thin, but all of it pointed towards California. Cravetts had enlisted in the California Column at Marysville, a small town north of Sacramento. The man who had bought Cravetts' ranch at Lordsburg told them he had given Cravetts a bankers draft on the Cattleman's Bank in San Francisco in payment for the place. The telegraph office clerk, anxious to help now in any way he could, came up with the information that Cravetts had often spoken of visiting San Francisco.

'Talked like he knowed the place real good,' he said.

It sure as hell wasn't much, Angel thought. But it would do.

Wells was up and about now, and he spent a lot of time with the Army telegraphers. Messages flew between Bowie and the Department of Justice in Washington. Reports had to be written, investigations set in hand, checks made. They sweated it out in the barren heat of

117

the Fort waiting for news and while they did, Wells started to unteach Frank Angel.

At first, Angel was sceptical.

'Listen to me, Frank,' Wells told him. 'You've been a fool for luck. Your luck ran out real fast when you came up against pros who knew you were coming after them. You've got to learn all over again. How to use a gun is one thing. How to use your head is another. So far you've been doing only the one. It's time to learn a few tricks.'

The first thing he did was to throw away the soft leather holster that Angel had bought in Silver City.

'Dammed dangerous rubbish,' Wells told him. 'You could snarl up you gun in a thing like that so bad you'd never even get it into action before they cut you to bits.'

He got an Army holster off one of the officers and went to work on it. First he cut away with a knife the flap all Army holsters had, and then he shaped the outer lip so that when the Army Colt was slid into the holster the trigger guard was completely exposed. Then he worked on the leather with saddle soap and dubbin until it was pliable, moulding the holster until it was shaped to the gun. He got a tape measure from the sutler and went to work measuring Angel's chest and waist and hips. Then he fashioned, clumsily using the clawed and paralysed right hand and cursing his own uselessness as he did so, a belt rig for the younger man. When he was finished he started in on a shoulder rig which could be used with the same holster. Then every day for a week he took the boy out on the flats at the far side of the Fort and had him practise drawing the gun. He showed him the standard gunfighter's repertoire: the fast draw from the hip, the shoulder-holster draw, the road-agent's spin, the border shift. Angel was a good pupil. His naturally fast reflexes adapted quickly to the new things Wells was teaching him and before long he was able to draw the Colt faster than

Wells' primitive timing device: a coin placed on the back
of the hand, held forward at arm's length was dropped to
the ground. As the coin was released, the draw was made.
Angel could draw and fire the unloaded sixshooter
before the coin hit the ground ten times out of ten, then
twenty times out of twenty.

'So far, so good,' Wells grunted. That was as close as he
came to praise. 'Now let's see about shooting.'

Day after day he ran through the full range of tests
that he himself had to pass every six months as part of his
Justice Department proficiency tests. He would make
Angel ride past on horseback at full gallop, firing at tin
cans set along a fence. He would throw the cans into the
air, as high as he could, making Angel turn his back.
Then he would rap out the command 'go!' and the boy
would wheel around and try to hit the cans in flight. He
showed him some of the ways to get out from under an
already drawn gun, the few he knew.

'By and large,' he drawled, grinning, 'there isn't any
way to beat the drop. A man has a loaded gun pointed at
you, all you can do is stand very still. Wait for your
moment, hope one comes. If it doesn't . . .' He shrugged.
'Let's hope it never happens,' he said grimly, gesturing
with the shattered right hand and tapping his crooked
leg with the cane he had to use.

Then when they had finished, they started all over
again. He told Angel about fanning a gun, and why most
times it was a damned stupid thing to do. He gave him
long lectures about hideaway guns, Derringers and over-
and-unders, pepperboxes and belt pistols, boot guns and
guns hanging from cords around the neck, tiny guns
capable of being hidden in the pockets of a man's vest
and big guns attached to the belt on metal swivels and
hooks. He told him about Derringers on elastic cords
hanging down sleeves, pocket pistols hidden between the

thighs or inside hard hats. And then they moved on to rifles.

Wells gave Angel a complete grounding in them all. Matchlocks and wheellocks, snaphaunces and Baltic locks, dog locks and flintlocks, breechloaders and revolving cylinders. Between themselves and all the officers they came up with a motley collection of weapons and Wells made Angel use them all. There was a huge old Hawken muzzle loader nearly as long as Angel himself, and there was a Remington Rolling-block that the Commanding Officer used for hunting.

Running flat out and firing as he ran, lying down and carefully sighting, using the guns on horseback or flat on his belly in the scrub until his shoulders were a mass of aching muscles and his ears rang constantly with the flat sound of the explosions, Frank Angel used them all: the Henry and the Spencer and the sweetest of them all, the Winchester '66. He learned the differences between them, too. The Winchester's lack of punch and range, the Henry's limited magazine capacity, the terrible power of the singleshot Sharp's 'Big Fifty' – all these he knew and understood, all of them Wells made him field-strip and reassemble, load and fire until he became not merely proficient but as close to perfect shooting as Wells felt he could in the time they had. 'That's it with the guns,' he said, one day. 'Now you've got to learn when not to use them.'

He gave Frank Angel a good and comprehensive understanding of the laws of the United States. Territorial law, Federal law, Army standing orders, the powers of the District Attorneys, the judges, the law officers. He explained the difference between a town marshal, who was a freelance town-tamer hired by a town to keep the place relatively law-abiding, men like Tom Smith who had run Abilene, or Hickok, whom Angel had once – it seemed like years ago – met, and the United States Marshal whose position was a Federal appointment and who was responsible for the maintenance of Federal law throughout an entire State or Territory. He told Angel about the powers of sheriffs, and their antecedence in old English common law, and the grand juries, whose antecedence was the same. The formation of the police forces of cities and their duties, the enormous number of ways in which civilian lawyers could ensure that a criminal known to be guilty by the officers of the law was never brought to trial. He explained all this and much more in simple, easily understood terms, and when Angel grew restive, impatient at so much talk, so little action, he would then tell him why it was necessary to know all this.

'You go after Cravetts with a gun in your hand the way you did before,' he said, 'and when you get him they'll hang you.'

'I'll give him an even break,' muttered Angel, 'which is more than he gave the Gibbonses.'

'No way,' Wells told him, shaking his head. 'You got to have a warrant for the man's arrest, a reason for trying to take him. He killed someone, then there's a warrant for his arrest wherever he did it.'

'Except a Kansas warrant isn't any damned use at all in California,' Angel said bitterly. 'So my way is the only way.'

'Frank,' Wells said, 'you haven't been listening. Federal law isn't hampered by State or Territorial borders. . . .'

'I forgot,' Angel said, 'you got a warrant on Cravetts for that Army payroll robbery.'

'Which is a Federal offence,' Wells nodded.

'I forgot,' Angel repeated. 'I only want him for what happened at the Gibbons place.'

121

'I know that,' Wells said. 'But we've got to do it my way, Frank. You can't take the law into your own hands.'

'Can't I?' Angel said darkly, and slouched out of the room into the darkness of the ramada outside. Wells let him go. The inaction was plaguing Angel. Dammit, he thought, it isn't making me any more even-tempered. What in the name of sweet charity was the Department doing, taking so long getting word to them? Ah, he thought, it takes time. Finding one man in a city who had no reason at all to conceal his presence there was difficult enough. Finding a man who had every reason not to want to be found ... he shook his head, knowing what the Department, with its limited resources, was facing. They would check everything. Hotel registers, boarding houses, laundries, electors' lists, newspapers, shipping line passenger lists, directory publishers, process servers, anyone who kept records. But it took time, and time was on Cravetts' side. The longer they took to get a lead on him, the more likely it was that they would never get one.

Two days later word came in: they had run down Lee Monsher in San Francisco.

EIGHTEEN

San Francisco!

Wells and the man from the District Attorney's office who met them at the Ferries were busy exchanging information almost from the moment they clapped eyes on one another and hardly seemed to notice the swarming, astonishing city. Frank Angel regarded it all wide-eyed: it was the first city he had ever been in, and everything was on such a scale as to make it an astonishing experience. The forests of masts in the harbour, growing it seemed thicker and taller as the ferry had brought them across the bay, the humps and hills of the town covered as far as the eye could see by one-storey houses in all colours, white and yellow, red and pink and blue, a chiarocscuro of hues that became in the bright sunlight a sort of bright and misty pale blue, beautiful against the green of the hills. Closer to, it was something else. Opposite the ferries were the cheap saloons and eating houses, boot-black stands, peanut vendors, newspaper sellers, candy men, stalls selling shrimp and crab and lobster, and over them all a clamour of noise such as Angel had never encountered. They walked up Market Street past buildings which gradually became more imposing, more permanent. Row upon row of substantial edifices of one, two, sometimes three storeys height marched along the busy downtown streets while behind them up the hills stretched serried rows of wooden houses running over the top of the heights and down the other side. The D.A.'s man, whose name was Larry James, told them that San Francisco now had a population of over 200,000 and it seemed to Angel as if everyone of them was on the streets. Well-dressed men in stovepipe hats jostled for space on the sidewalks with roughly-dressed miners. bearded sailors with bright blue-striped jerseys whistled and nudged each other when ladies dressed in the height of fashion paraded past them on the plank side-walks, their skirts daintily lifted to avoid the filthy water which spurted up between the boards as men clumped past. The streets were muddy and potholed and carriages dashing by often threw up a great splash of water that spattered passers-by or carriages going in the opposite direction with a fine spray of mud. Barouches, surreys, coaches, wagons thronged Market Street, and outside the shops and stores hung trays displaying ribbons and cloth for dresses. There were signs at every level the eye moved so that in the end one saw nothing. They passed palatial marble edifices, some of them looking like Angel's idea of a Doge's palace, which James told them were banks, or office buildings, or, once in a while, broth-els where, he said, only the finest food and liquor, only the most beautiful young women were to be found.

'You have to see the other side of the town, too, of course,' James remarked. 'We've got dives down on Pacific Street that would make a Wichita deadfall look like a rest home.'

But Angel hardly heard him. The city had taken him by the heart, the glamour, the people, the excitement, the pace of it grabbed his imagination. All he could think of was going out on the streets, walking around, seeing it, touching it, hearing it, smelling it, getting to know the secret corners of it. He watched the people going by. So many Chinese! So many nationalities: there a swart Mexican, trousers flared and conchoed like a Tijuana dandy, there an English sailor with a bright cheery face, a red handkerchief knotted beneath his chin, over there a coal miner in blue dungarees and an old shiny black coat, his eyes rimmed by the black rings of coaldust. Outside one building he saw men looking at a notice-board marked 'Help wanted' and saw requisitions for milkers and buttermakers and coachmen, tree fellers and day labourers. He soaked in all these things and many more as they made their way along Market Street and turned right into Post Street. When they were settled in James' office, he got out a folder with some papers in it and spread them out on his desk for Wells to see. Wells read the reports of the police investigators and nodded.

'Where is he now?' was all he said.

'He's got a suite at the Occidental – that's on Montgomery,' James said.

'A suite?' Wells raised his eyebrows.

'He's a big spender,' James said. 'Must be one of the best customers they've had on the Barbary Coast for years. Every cardsharp, every brothel – they've all had a piece of our friend's money.'

'The US Army's money, you mean,' Wells gently reminded him.

James grinned. 'You can't say the Government isn't getting it's money's worth,' he said.

'How have you played it?' Wells wanted to know.

'Got a two-man tail on him,' James said. He was a compactly-built blond-haired man of about thirty, with a neatly-trimmed moustache he stroked often with the back of his forefinger. 'Twenty-four hours a day.'

'He hasn't contacted anyone who looks like our man?'

James shook his head.

'Sorry, boys,' he said, spreading his hands. 'This Cravetts fellow just hasn't showed his face once. May not even be here.'

'One way to find out,' Wells said flatly. James looked his question as the Justice Department man got heavily to his feet. 'Let's ask Monsher. What name's he using, by the way?'

'Lee,' James said. 'Robert Lee.'

'Cheeky bastard,' Wells said.

They had it all neatly set up and James took Monsher as he came down into the lobby.

'Step right this way, Monsher,' he said quietly. 'And don't make any fuss.' He emphasized the suggestion with a nudge of the barrel of his pocket pistol in Monsher's ribs. It was smoothly done and no one in the crowded lobby even looked up. Monsher's head came up at James' words and his eyes swiftly moved left and then right, his weight shifting on the balls of his feet.

'Before you try it,' James said dryly, 'look over by the desk.'

He let Monsher see Wells and Frank Angel. They were no more than ten feet away. Their hands were in the pockets of their coats.

'Now the door,' James nodded. Monsher looked there, and the deputy leaning against the doorpost nodded. He had a mackinaw folded over his arm. His hand was concealed beneath it.

'There's another man outside,' James said. 'So don't bother thinking about running for it. Just relax and come along quietly.'

Monsher's shoulders fell about two inches, and then he turned and smiled at James, spreading his arms wide and saying 'Mister, you sure you got the right man? Mah name's Lee, Robert Lee.'

'Yeah, and this is Appomattox,' James said. He gave Monsher a shove with the barrel of the gun. 'Move!'

Monsher protested again, a little louder this time.

Heads turned in the lobby and Monsher laughed, no sound coming from his mouth.

'You're in trouble, lawman,' he hissed. 'You cain't shoot me in heah, now can you?'

'Don't bet on it,' Wells said, limping across to hear the last words. 'I wouldn't mind having the chance.'

'Well, well, well,' Monsher said quietly. 'Done said we shoulda kilt you.'

'You sure as hell tried,' Wells said coldly. 'Let's go, Monsher.'

Again Monsher laughed without sound and then suddenly he whirled around and shouted 'Help! These men are trying to rob me!'

He shortarmed Wells away from him, and the big man reeled off-balance, his cane slithering away from him on the parquet floor. Monsher ran a few steps towards a group of men, still shouting that they were trying to rob him, and someone laid a restraining arm on James' hand as he went to pursue the man. He tried to shake off the men crowding around him now asking questions, and Monsher darted across the lobby as he saw the deputy by the doorway push forward, losing his indolent air, the mackinaw falling discarded on the floor. A woman screamed as she saw the heavy revolver in the deputy's hand and then people were scattering away from Monsher and James fought clear of the men around him, his pistol out and ready but unable to fire because of the milling, shouting crowd of people. Monsher went straight across the lobby at a dead run and hit the windowframe with his head tucked down against his right shoulder, going through the whole thing in a smashing crash of flying woodwork and glass, the sheer shocking noise of the impact stopping people as if they had frozen for a second, and in that second those standing close to Frank Angel saw his hand start to move and then lost it because the gun that was in his hand blared a shot and Monsher seemed to falter in mid-air as he went through the window and hit the sidewalk outside, rolling off it into the muddy street. Men shouted hoarsely outside and a horse whinnied, shying away from the mudcoated thing that came up in front of it in the street.

Monsher was trying to stand but his right leg wouldn't support him and he clawed inside his jacket, swearing at the mudslick hands that hampered him, the heavy gun coming out of the shoulder holster as Angel came through the shattered window and then threw himself face down on the soaking sidewalk as Monsher's bullet whacked a chunk of wood out of the wall of the hotel. People were scattering off the street, men shouting warnings to each other as Monsher managed to gain his footing, throwing shots towards the window from which he had exited and keeping everyone down on the sidewalk as he lurched across the street and into the dark shadows of Sutter Street. James came out of the doorway of the hotel, his men with him, and then they ran straight across the open street towards where Monsher had disappeared and even as Angel got to his feet, his mouth framing a warning shout, there was a lance of flame from the darkness and one of the two deputies ploughed sideways, face down dead in the mud of Montgomery Street. James leaped to the sheltering sidewalk outside the Lick House where astonished faces peered through the windows fronting the street and the other deputy as if on signal diverged to the opposite side of Sutter. Then the two of them eased around the corner, using the shadows. There was no shot. Angel was across the street by now and he went straight past James, out in the middle of the street.

He had counted Monsher's shots and knew the man's gun was empty. Monsher would not take time to reload. He would be running for safety and if they lost him now, then he could go to ground again, one face among two hundred thousand. James shouted something behind him but Frank Angel ran straight on past the lighted windows in Sutter, then stopped in the middle of the street. Monsher was gone.

James came panting up behind him, then the other deputy.

'He can't have gone far,' Angel said. 'I hit him in the right leg.'

The deputy looked at Angel. 'You what?' he said.

'I hit him in the right leg. Just above the knee.'

'How the hell do you know that?' the deputy said.

'That was where I aimed,' Angel told him, as if the explanation was unnecessary. The deputy looked at Larry James, who shrugged.

'Take the right hand side, Tom,' he told the man. 'Check every saloon, everywhere that's open. If Angel here wounded him, he can't have gone far. I'll take the left side.' He turned around to face the small crowd which was assembling about twenty feet behind them. 'You people get off the street!' he shouted. 'The shooting isn't over yet!' There was some muttering and the crowd melted back slightly, but their curiosity was stronger than their fear. As James went into the first saloon on Sutter, they clustered around near the doors and windows, trying to see inside. Angel did not follow James. He went directly for the first corner along the street, a brightly-lit and bustling thoroughfare. A sign told him it was Kearny Street. There were fashionably-dressed people everywhere. There was a crippled man selling newspapers on the corner.

'You see a man come running – well, limping, maybe

– past here a few minutes back? Tow-haired guy, about my height?'

'Lissen, Mac, you wanna paper? What I do is sell papers, see, not hand out information, right?'

Angel said: 'Here's a dollar. Now—'

'Blood all over his leg, face all cut, covered in mud?' chirped the newsvendor. 'Sure, he went into Kennedy's over the street there.'

Angel sloshed through the muddy puddles to the far side of the street and pushed in through the swinging doors. The place was done out in high style. Mahogany bar, polished glass shelves, ornate mirrors, curtained booths – some with the curtains drawn – and a pianist at the far end of the room playing rinkytink music. Above the room was a gallery with tables and chairs that ran on both sides and across the far end above the pianist's head. Angel saw the dark spots on the floor but he did not react. He walked to the bar and leaned on it, feeling the pulse in the air, the knowledge that Monsher was there. About twenty people in the place, Angel guessed. Scattered around, not bunched.

'Give me a beer,' he told the bartender. The man nodded and pulled the beer, scooping the foam off the top with a wooden spatula. His eyes skittered around, never meeting Angel's. Once they flickered up towards the balcony above the pianist's head. Angel could see the fear in them. He leaned on the bar. The skin on his neck and back crawled. He was a sitting duck if Monsher decided to take him. He moved along the bar a little until he was about six or seven feet from the pianist, then turned casually and leaned with his back to the bar, watching the man play. The piano was old and well worn, the keys yellowed and scarred by what looked like many cigar and cigarette burns. They looked like brown thumbprints. Angel saw another one appear as he watched and the pianist jerked nervously, missing the beat. He felt, rather than saw, the pistol barrel poking through the rails of the balcony and went headlong for the spot he had picked out a few minutes before. There were tables and chairs at this end of the room, most of them unoccupied. He moved in a long low running dive as the gun spoke and then hastily spoke again, tearing a great chunk out of the top of the mahogany bar with the first shot and then smashing into the filthy boards of the floor behind Angel as he got beneath the marble topped table and slid his own gun out from the shoulder holster. He could wait: Monsher was losing blood, James would have heard the shots. He wanted to get up and kill Monsher. At the same time he knew that if he did, they would never learn where Cravetts had gone. All this went through his head in the seconds that followed his dive beneath the table. He eased to where he could see the upstairs balcony and at the same moment a woman screamed and he saw Monsher stand up at the rail of the balcony with his gun levelled aiming at the door. Angel saw Larry James and the deputy behind him come to a halt in the middle of the empty gangway as Monsher grinned and eared the hammer of the gun back and then Angel came out from beneath his table and fired in one continuing movement, his bullet taking Monsher high on the left side of his chest and hurling him shouting with pain backwards out of sight. Angel kept on moving and bounded up the stairway to the balcony, hearing James come pounding up behind him. Monsher was lying between two tables and some overturned chairs, cursing weakly and trying to lift the gun to fire again. Angel kicked it out of his hand.

'Damn you!' Monsher spat. The top of his pants leg was wet with blood and another stain was mushrooming at his left side. Monsher's forehead was wet with sweat, but his eyes were alive and full of hate. There were cuts on his face and hands.

'Damn you!' he said again. 'Done said we shoulda—'

'Killed me, you said that before,' Angel said coldly. 'Can you walk?'

Monsher shook his head.

'Then we'll carry you,' Angel said. 'Just a minute, James.'

Gun still canted ready he bent over the fallen man and without haste went over the possible hiding places for weapons that Wells had taught him. From a pocket stitched on the inside of the man's jacket where a pocket would normally have been he produced a neat and deadly little snubnosed Derringer, and on a loop of rawhide around Monsher's neck there was a thin-bladed knife in a soft leather sheath.

'Quite an arsenal.' James remarked.

'It figured,' Angel said. 'Where is Cravetts, Monsher?'

'Go straight to hell,' Monsher told him.

Angel knelt down and laid hold of Monsher's right ankle. Without warning he turned the man's leg sharply. Monsher's head went back and he screamed like a horse going over a cliff.

'Jesus!' he sobbed, the colour gone from his face, his eyes burning and full of agony in the dark hollows of his head. 'Holy Jesus!'

'I asked you a question.'

There was no sympathy in Frank Angel's voice, no reaction to the sharp scream of pain Monsher had uttered. Larry James started to say something but Angel silenced him with a look. James turned uncomfortably and nodded a signal to his deputy. The man eased down the stairway and towards the door. Angel did not notice him go, or if he did he made no effort to stop him.

'I – said – rot in hell, you shit-faced—'

Again Angel twisted the wounded leg sharply, and again Monsher's words ended in a scream of pain. He looked whey-faced now. Sweat was pouring down his drawn visage, and matting his tow hair. His fingers scrabbled on the dirty boards of the floor. His eyes told the story of what he would do to Angel if he could get up. But his left arm was now hanging limp and flaccid, and the oozing blood was slowly draining Monsher of his strength. His eyelids drooped.

'Where is Cravetts?' Angel repeated inexorably.

Monsher shook his head and without expression Angel laid hold of the wounded leg again. This time however Monsher gasped and tried to sit up, his right hand extended and a pleading expression on his face.

'No,' he said. 'Not again.'

'Talk then.'

'Dick – headed for Virginia City,' Monsher said.

'You're lying!' Angel snapped. He gripped Monsher's ankle hard and Monsher shouted out in panic.

'No – it's the truth! You—' he rolled over to look at Larry James. 'Get him away from me! He'll cripple me!'

'What a good idea,' Angel said pleasantly. He gave a slight twist and the sweat beads jumped on Monsher's forehead. 'You're supposed to be a lawman!' cried Monsher. 'Get him off me – he's out of his skull!'

'Listen, Angel . . .' James began. Then he saw Frank Angel's eyes and lapsed into silence. He turned to check the doorway. Where the hell was Wells?

'What about Torelli?' Angel asked the man on the floor.

'I'll tell you . . . but you got to promise . . . get me to a hospital.'

'I promise,' Angel said. 'Torelli.'

'Took a boat to New York,' Monsher said. His strength was going faster now, like bathwater getting shallower, running quicker.

'Why did Cravetts go to Virginia City?' Angel wanted to know.

'Parlay his stake,' Monsher gasped. 'Saloon. Going to buy . . . saloon. Listen—' his hand reached out and clutched Angel's sleeve. 'You promised. Hospital. You promised . . .'

'That's right,' Angel said. He straightened up.

'You can have him,' he told James.

James looked down at the bleeding man on the floor. Monsher was pretty well unconscious now. There was a heavy pool of blood beneath his body. 'You gave him a hard time, Angel,' he said.

'Poor chap,' was the reply. 'You believe what he said?'

'I believe him,' James said. The door of the saloon burst open and Wells came clumping in with the deputy who had been sent to fetch him. He saw the two of them standing on the balcony.

'Is he dead?' he shouted up.

'All but,' James told him.

'Get anything out of him?' Wells asked Angel.

'All we need to know,' Frank Angel told him.

The deputy hustled some men off the street and requisitioned a blanket from one of the stores on Kearny. There was a crowd outside the saloon but they soon dispersed when Monsher's body was brought out cradled in the blanket and put into a paddy wagon.

'I'll take him downtown, sor,' the deputy told James.

'See he gets those wounds looked at,' James shouted after the rattling wagon splashed off down Kearny. The deputy waved an arm in acknowledgement and the three men stood on the pavement by Kennedy's for a few minutes, Wells lighting a cigar and puffing on it reflectively.

'Virginia City,' he said, musing. 'That's a hard ride.'

Then he shrugged. '*Que sera* . . . we'll skin out tomorrow morning. Larry, can you get us a room someplace for the night?'

'Already did,' James grinned. 'At the Occidental.'

'You mean—'

'While we were waiting for Monsher,' the DA's man said. 'Figured Monsher sure as hell wasn't going to be needing it.'

Wells shook his head grinning and they started back along Sutter to the hotel. Later they ate some cold chicken and Angel tasted white wine for the first time in his life.

'You handled things . . . uh, pretty good,' Wells said, finally.

Angel nodded, keeping his head bent over the plate.

'But you're still pushing your luck,' the older man grumbled.

For the first time since they had left Fort Bowie, Frank Angel smiled. It made his whole face boyish again.

'Hell, Angus,' he said. 'Isn't that what luck is for?'

Wells had no answer for that one. They finished their meal and went up to their room.

'Virginia City,' Wells muttered as he turned in. 'He's sure as hell got his nerve.' He fell asleep almost instantly, leaving Angel still dressed sitting at the window looking out across the lighted city.

When he woke up next morning the boy was gone.

NINETEEN

Angel was moving fast.

Lake Tahoe stretched ahead of him, forty miles wide and blue as a Chinaman's robe. Quail scattered in front of his horse, their head feathers quivering with every movement as they ran between bushes and rocks. Ahead, the mountains soared in huge phalanxes of black and puce and purple and slate, their shoulders mantled with pine, peaks etched with snow. Angel pointed the sorrel's nose downhill from the pass.

'Well, there's the avalanche,' he muttered to the horse, 'but where's the trail?'

In truth, the trail along the flank of Echo Mountain was like an avalanche to look at, a series of gigantic furrows scoured into the flinty earth by the wheels of the Concords and wagons on their way to and from the mining country. He followed it down to the shore of the lake and by nightfall he was over Second Summit and coming down the long shelving slope eastwards into the Nevada desert. He wondered what Wells was doing.

He had left no note. Wells wouldn't need to be told where Angel was going, and a frosty smile touched Angel's lips as he visualised the older man stomping around the hotel room cursing when he discovered him gone. But he knew Wells would waste very little time on

recrimination. He would move heaven and earth to get
to Virginia City, to cut down the head start Angel had
given himself. He figured he had a slight edge on the
Justice Department man but nothing more. Travelling
horseback he could make better time than the coach
Wells would have to use. That might give him twenty four
hours at the best, twelve hours at the worst, to find
Cravetts in Virginia City. He shrugged to himself. It
would just have to be enough.

Next morning early he pushed up the twisting road
that climbed the canyon to Mount Davidson, passing
dump after deep mine dump, and shaft houses either
working or already abandoned and rusted. Then just like
that, around a corner he was in the town, its crude, ugly,
overpowering mass clamped to the face of the canyon.
The streets went up the side of the hill in lettered array,
with downhill streets crossing them. Everywhere there
were shacks and tinpot stores with mining equipment
hanging in jangling disarray outside them. The sidewalks
were crammed with people, and the whole length of B
Street was one churning seething hive of animals and
men, carts and wagons and coaches and horses and
mules and yapping dogs and over it all lay a steady, unal-
tering level of noise – the deep thumping of the pile
drivers below ground, the unending hubbub of human
voices, and the punctuation provided by the shrill blast
of the Virginia & Truckee Railroad down at the depot.

It was already growing very hot in the open. The light
mountain air was thin and heady. Angel found a livery
stable on the mountain side of B Street and while he was
unsaddling, asked the owner a question.

'Cravetts, Cravetts?' said the man, scratching his head.
'Cain't say I've heerd the name, son, but that ain't
nuthin'. Too danged many people hereabouts for a man
to know any but his own kin, an' a right few o' them ain't

usin' the name they had in the States.'

'Place is sure humming,' Angel agreed, looking out on to the street.

'Waal, we better make the best of her,' the stableman said. 'You want my 'pinion, the gold's a gonna peter out afore too long, an' the way they're drillin' down there, wouldn't surprise me 'f the whole burg caved right in.'

'Cheerful thought,' Angel said. 'Where's a decent hotel?'

'You could try the International down the street a ways,' he was told. 'Good as any. The stage line uses it.'

Angel thanked him and went out on the street, drifting with the endless crowd on the battered and broken sidewalks. Virginia City was raw and ugly and the smell of gold excitement came off it like rancid butter. Along the street he found whiskey mills every twenty paces, and looked into one or two. They were cheap deadfalls and he didn't expect to find anything, but he looked anyway. Wells had told him that. Always look, he said. Costs nothing, and you never know what you'll find. But there was nothing to find. He had been naive to think he could come to a big place like this and find one man in it. He walked further along the street, and in the slide area between two buildings he saw a cockfight with a crowd of men clustered around the screeching birds, fists full of currency, shouting and cheering when blood was spilled. He came to the International Hotel, a solid-looking brick building of two storeys, and went inside, taking a seat in the lobby. He was trying to think like Wells, and cast his mind back to their weeks of waiting at Fort Bowie. Wells had told him many of the ruses, the ploys he had used in his time with the Justice Department. Tricks of the trade, he'd called them.

'People become thieves because they're lazy,' Wells

138

had said. 'Deep down, basically, I mean. They're too lazy to graft for their money so they steal it instead. They'll kill while they're stealing it because they're too lazy to fight for what they've stolen. A lawman has to capitalize on the fact that criminals are lazy, greedy, cunning, always expecting someone to try and put something over on them. And use the knowledge to bring them to him.'

Angel nodded to himself. But how, Angus, how? He had to get action quickly. 'Always use the simplest, most direct methods,' Wells had told him. 'Less chance of fouling up on a detail.'

He went across to the desk.

'How would I go about finding a man named Cravetts who runs a saloon in town somewhere?' he asked.

The clerk looked at him indulgently.

'In Virginia City proper, sir,' he said, 'or Gold Hill?'

'I don't know.'

'There are more than one hundred saloons in town, sir,' the clerk said patiently.

'Which one is the biggest, the fanciest?' Angel asked.

The clerk raised one eyebrow slightly. 'The Alhambra, I'd say.'

'That's on B Street?'

'No, sir, on C, at the corner of Taylor. Two blocks along and one up.'

Angel nodded his thanks and left. He found the Alhambra without much difficulty, and pushed through the crowd to the bar. The bartender served him the beer he asked for and then pointed down the bar at a florid-faced man with a huge belly standing talking to some of his customers near the free lunch counter.

'Happy Jack's the owner, you want to talk to him,' he said as reply to Angel's question. Angel walked down to the end of the bar and waited for a moment until he caught Happy Jack's eye.

'Wondered if you could help me,' Angel said. 'I'm trying to contact someone. Name of Cravetts. Dick Cravetts. Bought a saloon up here quite recently.'

Happy Jack pursed his lips and looked at his moulded ceiling for inspiration. 'Cravetts,' he muttered. Then a beaming smile split his face wide open, instantly explaining his nickname.

'Dick Cravetts!' he said. 'Course! Bought that big place down on A Street next to Crazy Kate's. Had a fancy opening. Harry—' he called to the bartender, '—what did that guy Cravetts call the old Brewery when he took it over?'

'The Pay Roll,' said the bartender, and Happy Jack smiled, his double chins jiggling. 'Some name for a saloon, eh, mister—?'

'Torelli,' Angel told him. 'Frank Torelli.'

'You new in town, Frank?'

'Just got in,' Angel said. 'I'm at the International. Thought I'd look old Dick up.'

'Well, that's where you'll find him, down the hill all the way from here, turn left on A and there you are. Give him my regards, tell him to come in some time for a chinwag.'

He gestured at his double chins and the grin split his face again. 'Chinwag,' he gurgled. 'Get it?'

Angel supplied the fat man with laughter and a drink, then went out into the street and found his way back to the hotel, where he booked a room for the night. It was no problem to find someone to go down to the Pay Roll Saloon with his message.

'Just tell him Torelli, Frank Torelli sent you,' he told the youngster. 'Tell Mr Cravetts I'm in Room 14 at the International and I have to see him about the money.'

'See him about the money, yessir,' said the boy, and

picked the silver dollar that Angel flipped to him out of the air. With a satisfied nod Angel went into the dining room and ate a good meal. Then he went up the street and bought a few things which he took to his room. Once there he stripped off his coat and went to work. When everything was the way he wanted it, he sat down on an upright chair in the corner of the room to wait out the afternoon. He did not think anything would happen before dark.

They came soon after nightfall and if he had been in the bed he would have had no chance. The first one hit the rope Angel had rigged two feet off the floor and went sprawling as Angel dropped the second man with a roundhouse clout from the barrel of the Army Colt. The first man was getting to his knees when Angel hit him in the throat and dropped him retching beside his twitching comrade. Angel manhandled the man on to the bed and lashed him feet and hands X-shaped on the hard bed. Then he checked the pulse of the man by the door, nodding in satisfaction. The man would be out for an hour or more. He picked up the water jug from the wash stand and threw water into the face of the man on the bed. The man surged up spluttering against his restraining bonds and then realizing he was bound relaxed backwards on the bed, only his dark eyes alive with apprehension. The swarthy skin and heavy black moustache suggested foreign blood.

'What's your name?' Angel rasped.

The man tried to spit at him.

'I know Cravetts sent you,' Angel said. 'What for?'

The man turned his face away from his questioner, his mouth a tight thin line.

'All right,' Angel said, and hit him hard in the belly. The man's eyes bugged out of his head and he arched upwards on the bed, his mouth a gaping O of astonished pain. Then he retched and fell back panting, his eyes wide and filled now with fear.

'One more time,' Angel said, 'What were you supposed to do?'

The man shook his head. 'He'd kill me,' he said.

'You think I won't?'

Again the man shook his head. Angel said nothing more. He took one of the cartridges he had stood ready on the bureau, its leaden slug already extracted. He poured the gunpowder out on the top of the marble wash table making a long thin line. Then he touched a match to it. The powder lit with a small sound, and then burned smoking from one side of the table to the other. The man on the bed watched, a crease of puzzlement between his brows. Then Angel came across to the bed and ripped the man's shirt, exposing his bare body. He yanked the man's trousers and underpants down to his knees and without haste poured the powder from two more cartridges on the man's naked body, starting at the breastbone and letting the trail trickle down to the man's genitals. The man caught on now and surged against his bonds, shaking himself to make the powder spill off his body, but the perspiration kept most of it where Angel had poured it. Then Angel looked at the man and took a match from the box.

'Last chance,' he said.

The man's Adam's apple went up and down with a sound like a boot coming out of a mudhole.

'You wouldn't,' he ventured. The look on his captor's face stopped him saying more.

'Your name,' Angel said relentlessly.

'Bryan,' the man said. 'Barney Bryan.'

'Go on.'

'He said we was to kill you, that's all.'

'Just that? Go to the International and kill a man called Torelli?'

'That's all.'

'You're lying,' Angel said and struck a match.

'Christ, no, Torelli, lissen, I'll tell you!' screeched the man on the bed, panic in his expression. 'Put that thing out!'

Angel blew out his match.

'Talk,' he said.

'Cravetts said we was to bring you in. He said you couldn't be Torelli because Torelli was dead, so he wanted to know who you was.'

'Then what?'

'We was to bring you to his house. Up on D Street.'

'Describe it.'

'Big place, it is,' Bryan said. Now he was talking, the words flowed quickly. 'Big bay windows, wrought iron fence. Terraced steps an' them gingerbread gables on the roof. All painted white. It's the third house along from Union on the left.'

'Who's up there with him?'

Bryan shook his head. 'I don't know, Torelli, honest. I only been there the once.' The colour was coming back into his face now. He looked almost eager to please.

Angel turned away and spent ten good minutes lashing the hands and feet of the man on the floor with a length of rope. Then he grinned down at Bryan.

'Room's paid for,' he said. 'You might as well use it.'

Bryan watched him in silence as he put on his shoulder holster rig and donned his jacket.

'You – you goin' after Cravetts?' he said in disbelief.

Angel nodded.

'You mean – you set this up just to find out where he was?'

'Right,' was the monosyllabic reply. 'I couldn't take

143

him in the saloon.'

'You're out of your head,' Bryan said flatly. 'He'll cut your gizzard out an' feed it to the dogs!'

'That'll be the day,' Angel said, and went out.

TWENTY

Angel underestimated Angus Wells.

The Justice Department man wasted no time in recriminations. He knew where Angel had gone and why, so instead of cursing he used all his energy and all authority his office gave him to set up a chain of transportation. Within an hour of his discovery of Angel's disappearance, Wells was in a specially-chartered paddle steamer churning across San Francisco Bay. He had no eyes for the beauty of the scenery, fuming as Angel Island went by to starboard, fretting as they forged through San Pablo Bay and Benicia slipped astern. He was still grumbling with impatience as he stumped off the boat at Stockton and clambered aboard the waiting Concord.

He was no sooner in the red-painted stagecoach than the ribbonshaker gave vent to an explosive Rebel yell and the team careened out of the depot raising a huge cloud of dust as they burned up the road towards Sacramento.

A train was waiting for them there: Larry James had telegraphed ahead. It was just an engine with a flat car behind it, and had steam up already. They could only go as far as end of track, which meant that Wells had to pick up another Concord at Shingle Springs. He picked his way past the horde of gandy dancers shuffling gravel on to the newly-built right of way by the light of flaring kerosene lamps. Night was down hard now on the teeth of the Sierras, but Wells would brook no delay. Aching in every joint he piled into the waiting Concord and the driver swung out on to the Placerville road. They pulled in four hours later.

'What's the road like?' Wells asked the company at large, miners, travellers and freighters using the eating house on their way to or from the high country. He was wolfing down a plate of cold meat, beans and tortillas which he hardly tasted. It was fuel and Wells took it aboard as an engine takes on wood.

'Purt' good all the way,' one grizzled oldster said. 'Watered ever' night in summer, so she's hard as rock.'

'More or less,' another grinned. 'They's a few rough edges left.'

Wells left them laughing at the sally and limped to the truck bed that had been set aside for him in a room upstairs. They would call him at four, just before dawn. He looked at himself in the cracked mirror. His teeth shone whitely from the dusty grime of his face. He fell exhausted on the bed, fully dressed, his dreams haunted by the fear of being too late.

Dawn was streaking the eastern sky as, with a pistolcrack snap of his whip the driver yelled the team into motion, lurching down the flat empty road towards the distant mountains. By midday the road was full of wagons lumbering along behind their teams of oxen, coaches and carts going both east and west. Where it was possible they overhauled them, swerving out on to the wrong side of the road, sometimes heeling over dangerously into the thin ditches alongside it, but miraculously the driver kept them upright, whipping the horses into a sharp trot as they went uphill and lashing them into an all-out gallop when the road sloped downwards. Gradually the trail began to wind and turn more. Several times they hauled in hurriedly as they came around blind corners to find a strung-out ox-team on the far side, but the driver was one of the best and kept the coach rattling at a hell of a lick all the way up to Echo Summit Pass, where they changed teams.

If Wells even saw the astonishing sweep of mountains and valleys tumbling away at his feet like a map of the world he made no comment on it. He stretched his arms and stomped his feet to iron out the kinks from the hours in the coach, and climbed back aboard the moment the driver said he was ready.

Then they were off again like a bat out of hell, thundering along the flanks of Lake Tahoe and heading for the last divide on the Sierra, crossing the line into Nevada as dusk shrouded the far mountains with a purple cloak. They heaved to a clamorous stop outside the International Hotel in Virginia City at seven thirty, having cut almost twenty four hours off the normal journey from San Francisco. If Angus Wells was tired he gave no sign of it. A rapid-fire string of commands sent messengers running down B Street and within another twenty minutes Sheriff Jim Nisbet and two deputies were with Wells in the lobby of the hotel. Standing there in a tight knot, they listened as Wells tersely outlined his authority, his reasons for being in Virginia City, and what he wanted Nisbet and his men to do.

'No problem,' Nisbet said. 'Harry, get down to A Street and check whether Cravetts is there. Don't do anything. Just check. Come back here as fast as you can and report.'

The deputy nodded and went into the night running. Wells went across to the desk. The clerk looked at him with distaste.

'A room,' Wells said. The clerk frowned and then saw Sheriff Nisbet behind Wells. A smile pasted itself across his face.

'You look as if you have been travelling hard, sir,' he smirked.

'Some,' Wells said. 'What number?'

'I'll put you in number fifteen, sir,' the clerk said. 'A nice room on the first floor. Right next to Mr Torelli.'

Wells was turning away from the desk as these words were spoken, but he wheeled around and clamped both hands on the clerk's forearms. The man went white with fear and his eyes rolled for help towards the sheriff.

'Who?' shouted Wells. '*Who?*'

'Uh – ah – I – sir, you're hurting my arm.'

'What number is he in?' snapped Wells.

'Mr Torelli, sir? Number fourteen, but—'

His words trailed off as Wells headed for the staircase, the sheriff close behind him. The clerk looked at one of the deputies in astonishment.

'Is something wrong?' he said, tentatively.

'If it ain't,' said the man, 'it's about to be.'

TWENTY-ONE

The big house was lit up like a Halloween pumpkin.

Every window was ablaze with light, and through open french doors string music drifted sweetly out into the still summer night. The sidewalks on both sides of D Street were lined with carriages and surreys, and here and there their drivers stood by their horses awaiting their masters with that peculiarly listless air which is the mark of their profession.

'Is that the Cravetts place?' Angel asked one of them.

'Yessuh,' the negro said.

'Big party?'

'Unnerstand so, suh,' the man replied. 'Unnerstand so.'

Angel turned away, a smile of wintry devilishment touching the corners of his mouth. Cravetts was obviously playing the part of the rich man to the hilt.

'If the boys at Fort Riley knew what had happened to their pay checks they'd tear this place down,' he told himself, and walked into the hallway behind an elderly couple with white hair. The man was dressed in evening clothes, the woman in a long gown that smelled faintly of mothballs. The brightly-lit hall led to an open doorway where a maid took the woman's wrap and the man's cloak. Just inside the doorway, which led into a big room blazing with the light of a beautiful crystal chandelier and packed with people in formal clothes stood a tall negro in a frogged uniform. He bent to hear the name of the man in front of Angel then his deep voice boomed out.

'Mistuh an' Missus John Mackay!'

The man and woman descended the two steps and shook hands with the burly man waiting for them, his face wreathed in smiles. Angel smiled in anticipation. Cravetts was handsomely dressed in a black evening suit. An experienced eye would have noticed that one of the sleeves was cut wider than the other, to allow the Derringer strapped to the left wrist to slip easily from behind the ruffled lace cuffs. Cravetts looked immaculate and poised but his face went stone grey when the negro boomed out Angel's name. Angel went down the two steps and stood in front of Cravetts.

'*You!*' Cravetts said. His eyes shuttled around the room. Everywhere was the genteel hum of conversation. Waiters circulated with trays on which stood glasses of champagne. There was an agony of indecision in his eyes.

Then he turned on his heel and ran head down smashing into a man and sending him flying backwards against a table, which overturned with a splintering crash. Women screamed and men ran forward towards the fallen man as Angel tried to get past them, elbowing his way through the milling throng as Cravetts went out through a door on the far side of the room. As he ran through the room Angel heard a hoarse shout outside and got on to the street to see one of the negro drivers picking himself up out of the dust on D Street, cursing and shaking his fist at the carriage carreening twenty yards away around the corner into Union Street. His eyes bugged as he saw Angel kneel in one smooth movement with the Army Colt coming up out of the shoulder holster and level across his forearm, booming even as the man's eyes took in the long sweet swift movement. Angel's bullet hit the galloping horse just below the left ear and it slewed forward on its breast, smashing dead into the board sidewalk outside a hardware store, scattering passers-by in panic as the carriage keeled over in a long arc, throwing Cravetts into the street. He hit the ground hard, then rolled and got to his feet, running into an alley as Angel came sprinting around the corner of Union.

It was cat black in the alley. Angel stood for a moment trying to pick up the thump of Cravetts' feet, but heard nothing. Then down at the far end of the littered passageway he saw a light come on and a blowsy female voice squawled, 'Who the shit is that?'

Angel ran hard and fast on downhill in that direction, coming out at the far end on a shaly open slope that canted downhill towards the canyon road going into Gold Hill. There were more cribs and saloons at this end of town, and in the light from their windows he saw the bull-shape of Cravetts boring through the crowd on the sidewalk. He was heading for the dark open slopes below Mount Davidson. Once there he could disappear into the mountains, steal a horse, be out of the country by morning. Angel ran as if the hounds of hell were on his tracks. He saw Cravetts go by the fine false front of the firehouse, its gold-lettered legend glinting in the lights from the street: 'Liberty Engine Co.' it announced proudly. Cravetts slid around the side of the building, between it and a tall pine standing sentry over a pile of tailings which led upwards to the gaping black maw of an abandoned mine shaft. As Angel came around the side of the building, Cravetts drove him back with two shots that whacked great chunks of planking from the side of the building. Angel hit the dirt and stayed there, reloading, as the big man bounded off again up the slope and disappeared into the dark bowels of the empty mine. Angel cursed. Did Cravetts know a way through the mine? More than likely. These hills would be riddled like a rabbit warren with tunnels and abandoned shafts. He had to keep close on Cravetts' tail.

Back down the street he heard a growing commotion, the sound of voices rising like surf. Looking over his shoulder as he got up on the face of the tailings he saw a knot of people hurrying down the canyon road from the edge of town. Some of them were carrying pine-knot torches and in the uncertain light the man leading them looked familiar. That broken, stumping gait, the head bent determinedly forward – Wells? How in the name of God had he got here so fast? He shook his head.

'No you don't, Angus,' he said aloud and then set off carefully up the hill and into the entrance of the mine.

Inside it was as black as the hinges of Hades. Feeling his way along the walls, Angel kept his eyes closed tight to speed his adjustment to the pitch blackness. When he opened them, he could make out the larger looming blacknesses of ore wagons and pit props, and in the centre of the tunnel the faint gleam of rails. He found he was in a level passageway that ran straight ahead into the belly of the mountain. After a hundred yards or so of cautious advance, the rails stopped. He could see nothing ahead but deep and impenetrable blackness. He stood still, letting his other senses take control. No smell, no sound, nothing. Yet the hairs on the back of his neck prickled. Cravetts was near. Somewhere near.

He moved carefully forward, feeling his way around some timber props that ran upwards towards the invisible roof. Without warning his foot sloshed suddenly in a two-inch deep puddle and the moment the sound was made a huge flash blasted out from his right and he felt the air swell and move as the bullet went within an inch of his right temple. Angel gave a huge shout of simulated agony and sat down heavily in the puddle of water, thrashing his arms around and coming to rest on his belly. After a couple of moments he thought he heard the sound of a foot moving, the soft sibilance of carefully treading leather on sand. He breathed shallowly through his nose, keeping every muscle of his body still, his eyes probing the wall of darkness ahead of him. Then he heard a definite sound, the shift of a foot on gravel somewhere to the left. Cravetts had moved all that way without making a sound. The man must be like a cat on his feet, Angel thought.

Then he heard the sound he had been hoping for. A dry, whispering sound a little like a rattler giving its first warning – the sound of a match being taken from a box. Then the match flared and simultaneously Cravetts saw Angel moving and fired in the same instant that Angel's Army Colt boomed. The muzzle flames lit the whole cavern for a second and Angel heard Cravett's bullet smack meatily into the wall, bringing down a small shower of dirt from the roof overhead. Angel's bullet turned Cravetts around to the left and smashed him against the wall, the gun spinning from the man's hand. Cursing in a huge bellowing roar, a bull taunted to its limits by the banderilleros, Cravetts tried to get to his feet but Angel's shot had gone right through the big meaty muscles of the upper thigh and Cravetts' left leg would simply not obey him. He levered himself into an upright sitting position as Angel came across the tunnel in a low, seeking, instinctive dive, shaking the Derringer loose as the younger man's shoulder crashed into his chest, slamming Cravetts back against the wall without a breath left in his lungs. Angel hauled the man half upright again

153

and smashed the edge of his hand across Cravetts' upper lip. Cravetts' head went back against the stone wall with a flat dull sound and then he slid over half unconscious in the dirty clay of the mine. Angel stood up wearily, his muscles trembling. Groping around, he found the box of matches and struck one. He kicked the Derringer away from Cravetts' reach and then saw a pine torch stuck into a bracket at an angle on the wall near the timber supports. He lit the torch and looked down at Cravetts, whose face and body were matted with clay-coloured dirt, his beautiful suit and white shirt spattered and filthy. Coursing sweat cut rivulets through the muck on his forehead. The light of hating madness was in the haunted eyes.

'Get it over with then, damn you!' screeched Cravetts.

Angel looked at him, then at the Army Colt in his own hand. It still had four bullets in it. He cocked the hammer. The triple click sounded like thunder in the enclosed tunnel.

'Go on, do it, do it!' yelled Cravetts. 'You've dogged me all across the country. Now do what you came after me for!' Angel pointed the long barrel at Cravetts. The man looked eagerly into the bore of the gun.

'Go ahead,' he shouted. 'Kill me, damn you!'

Far off, Angel caught a sound on the edge of his consciousness. It was as if he had faintly heard the surf breaking on some distant coast. He knew it then for what it was, the sound of a crowd coming up the hill. His skin crawled with the urge to kill Cravetts.

'Don't you want to know why?' he said quietly. 'Why I tracked you all across the country – why I came after you at all – why I'm going to kill you?'

'Who knows?' Cravetts seethed. 'Who cares? Must be a thousand people want me dead, boy. Go ahead and pull the trigger. Shoot, damn you!'

He watched with widening eyes as Angel let the gun down, uncocked it, and put it back into the shoulder holster.

'What are you, some kind of yellow half-breed?' screeched Cravetts. 'Can't you even pull a trigger, you chicken-livered sonofabitch?'

Angel shook his head, letting a soft smile touch his lips.

'You're going to hang, Cravetts,' he said quietly.

'Kill me, damn you! God rot your whey-faced soul – shoot me!' Cravetts slammed his fists against the rock wall of the tunnel in frustration.

'Wells was right,' Angel mused aloud. 'You'd rather commit suicide than pay for what you did. Goddammit, Cravetts, you're not worth wasting a bullet on!'

Cravetts was still cursing his captor in a mindless monotonous scream when Sheriff Nisbet came running along the tunnel with a lantern held on high, two deputies behind him porting rifles. Angus Wells hobbled along behind them, his face streaked with sweat. He took in the whole scene with one sweeping, all-encompassing glance and then something like a smile touched his eyes. It had been a hard ride for Angus Wells, but he looked at this moment as if he didn't mind a bit.

'Angel,' he said levelly, 'you're looking good.'

Frank Angel smiled slowly. 'Angus,' he replied, 'I'm feeling good, too.'

Then they went out of there together.

This time they saw all of San Francisco.

They brought Cravetts down from the high country and a few days later put him, heavily manacled and guarded by two hefty deputy US Marshals on a train bound for Kansas City, where he would be tried. Monsher, fully recovered now, went on a train the following day.

In questioning Cravetts, a further aspect of the man's amoral perfidy was revealed. When Angel asked him how he had known it was not Torelli asking for him in Virginia City, Cravetts had laughed.

'You got to picture it, Wells,' he said. 'I get a message saying Frank Torelli is in town and wants to see me. Now how can that be, I ask myself, because I killed Frank Torelli!'

He went on to tell them that he had murdered Torelli because the man's nerve was completely broken and he knew he would never be able to keep his mouth shut back East. He had dumped the body in San Francisco Bay, bought a ticket in Torelli's name for the New York clipper, made sure his name was on the passenger manifests, then simply thrown the ticket away. He had taken Torelli's share of the robbery money and used it to set himself up in style in Virginia City.

'In fact if I hadn't been throwing that party that night, I'd have taken care of you myself, Angel,' Cravetts had grinned, totally unrepentant. 'I'd have fixed your wagon. But I had to stay at the house to meet my guests.'

Now with duty done, reports filed, answers received, queries replied to, they set out to do the town. Wells said that there was some kind of reward from the Army, and that he figured the Justice Department could advance Angel some pin money. Angel needed no prompting to get himself fitted up for a good broadcloth suit and some shirts, underwear, socks, soft leather boots. He hired a handsome barouche and a fine pair of trotters and Larry James showed them his city, proud of it as any San Franciscan is, displaying all the jewelled facets of 'the most beautiful city on the American map', to his friends. They ate heathen food in Chinatown, using chopsticks, drinking rice wine served by giggling Chinese girls. They went out to the Cliff House and had drinks on the wooden balcony overhanging the sea, watching the seals on the rocks offshore through telescopes provided by the management. James introduced them to the Barbary Coast, where broad-bosomed madams received them in regal splendour in houses that would not have disgraced railroad tycoons. They ate crab and lobster and shrimp at waterside places in Sausalito, a little fishing village across the Bay.

They tried the fancy French cooking on Nob Hill, and they climbed to the top of Telegraph Hill one clear day to see the lovely wide panorama of the city below them and the bright blue Bay beyond.

They talked and talked, James telling them about the early days in San Francisco, and about Junipero Serra and Yerba Buena before that. He told them about the forty-niners and the vigilantes, and his memory of the crowds in the streets to see the first Pony Express rider thunder up Market Street and unsaddle outside the Wells Fargo offices on Grant.

The time slipped swiftly away, and then word came through on the telegraph that the date of the trial had been fixed. They packed their things and met Larry James for a last drink on the porch of the hotel.

'What will you do – afterwards, Frank?' the DA's man asked.

Angel watched the traffic going by on Montgomery Street for a while in silence, then shrugged.

'I guess I haven't anywhere to go now,' he said. 'I'll look for something when I get back to Kansas.'

James opened his mouth to say something then closed it abruptly as he caught the signal in Wells' eye.

'Ever been to Washington, Frank?' Wells asked artlessly.

'Washington DC? No, I haven't,' Angel replied.

'You could ride with me,' Wells said. 'Be glad of the company.'

'Hell, Angus,' Angel said. 'What would I do in Washington?'

'Few people there I'd like to have you meet.'

Angel emptied his beer glass and put it down on the table.

'Like who?' he asked.

'Attorney-General of the United States for one,' Wells said. 'Fact is, he told me specifically to bring you back. Wants to meet you.'

'Meet me? What for?'

'Who knows, Frank?' Larry James said. 'Maybe he wants to offer you a job. With the Department.'

'Oh, sure,' Angel grimaced. 'I can see it now.'

'Good job, Special Investigator with the Department,' Wells said.

'All expenses paid,' James added. 'See the country as well as serve it.'

'Pension when you're sixty-five,' James added.

'If you live to collect it,' grinned Wells.

'Washington's mighty pretty this time of year.'

'All those orange blossoms.'

'Fish for catfish in the Potomac.'

'Hey, hold on there,' smiled Angel, holding up a hand. 'You boys are working awfully hard. What is this, some kind of conspiracy?'

'I guess you could say it was that all right,' Wells grinned even wider. 'I reckon you'd be one of the best men the Department ever had.'

'Amen to that,' James said.

'Lots of pretty girls in the Justice Department offices,' Wells said.

Frank Angel grinned.

'That does it, boys,' he said. 'When do we leave?'

'Tomorrow,' Wells said, 'I already got you a ticket.'

Frank Angel just looked at him. Then they all burst out laughing.